THE GRAPHIC NOVEL

illustrated by
Tony Leonard Tamai
with Alex Niño

script by
Arthur Byron Cover

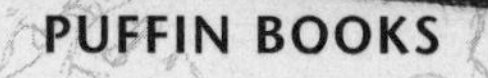
PUFFIN BOOKS

PUFFIN BOOKS
Published by the Penguin Group
Penguin Young Readers Group,
345 Hudson Street, New York, NY 10014 U.S.A.
Penguin Group (Canada), 90 Eglinton Avenue East, Suite 700,
Toronto, Ontario, Canada M4P 2Y3 (a division of Pearson Penguin Canada Inc.)
Penguin Books Ltd, 80 Strand, London WC2R 0RL, England
Penguin Ireland, 25 St. Stephen's Green, Dublin 2, Ireland
(a division of Penguin Books Ltd)
Penguin Group (Australia), 250 Camberwell Road, Camberwell, Victoria 3124,
Australia (a division of Pearson Australia Group Pty Ltd)
Penguin Books India Pvt Ltd, 11 Community Centre, Panchsheel Park,
New Delhi – 110 017, India
Penguin Group (NZ), Cnr Airborne and Rosedale Roads, Albany, Auckland 1310,
New Zealand (a division of Pearson New Zealand Ltd)
Penguin Books (South Africa) (Pty) Ltd, 24 Sturdee Avenue, Rosebank,
Johannesburg 2196, South Africa

Registered Offices: Penguin Books Ltd, 80 Strand, London WC2R 0RL, England

First published by Puffin Books, a division of Penguin Young Readers Group, 2005

10 9 8 7 6 5 4 3 2 1

A Byron Preiss Book
Byron Preiss Visual Publications
24 West 25th Street, New York, NY 10010

Additional art by Alex Niño
Lettering by Tony Leonard Tamai & Jeof Vita
Tones by Tony Leonard Tamai, Jeof Vita, Sherard Jackson, and Ernie Colon
Production assistance to Mr. Tamai: Katame Kajita, Yoshiteru Itou,
Kevin McCarthy, and Junko Suzuki
Series Editor: Dwight Jon Zimmerman
Series Assistant Editor: April Isaacs
Interior Design by M. Postawa & Gilda Hannah
Cover Design by M. Postawa

Puffin Books ISBN 0-14-240409-8

Printed in the United States of America

WILLIAM SHAKESPEARE'S
MACBETH

STARDATE: 1040. THE FORCES OF KING DUNCAN ARE ENGAGED IN BATTLE AGAINST THOSE OF THE REBEL MACDONWALD. LEADING THE CHARGE IS THE KING'S LOYAL SERVANT, THE THANE MACBETH.
WHEN SHALL WE MEET AGAIN? IN THUNDER, LIGHTNING, OR IN RAIN?

THOOM!!
WHEN THE HURLY-BURLY'S DONE, WHEN THE BATTLE'S LOST AND WON.
THAT WILL BE ERE THE SET OF SUN.
WHERE THE PLACE?
UPON THE HEATH.

DOOM!!
AHHH!
FAIR IS FOUL, AND FOUL IS FAIR. HOVER THROUGH THE FOG AND FILTHY AIR.

WHAT BLOODY MAN IS THAT?
HAIL BRAVE FRIEND. SAY TO THE KING THE KNOWLEDGE OF THE BROIL AS THOU DIDST LEAVE IT.
THE MERCILESS MACDONWALD SHOWED LIKE A REBEL'S WHORE. BUT ALL'S TOO WEAK.
BRAK!
CHIK!
FOR BRAVE MACBETH, WELL BE DESERVES THAT NAME, DISDAINING FORTUNE, WITH HIS BRANDISHED STEEL.

WHICH SMOKED WITH BLOODY EXECUTION LIKE VALOR'S MINION CARVED OUT HIS PASSAGE...
BLAM!
TILL HE FACED THE SLAVE...
WHIST!
WHICH NE'ER SHOOK HANDS NOR BADE FAREWELL TO HIM...

SHIING!!
KTHUNK!
TILL HE UNSEAMED HIM FROM THE NAVE AND FIXED HIS HEAD UPON OUR BATTLEMENTS.

O VALIANT COUSIN, WORTHY GENTLEMAN!
I AM FAINT, MY GASHES CRY FOR HELP.
SO WELL THY WORDS BECOME THEE AS THY WOUNDS. THEY SMACK OF HONOR BOTH. GO GET HIM SURGEONS.
WHO COMES HERE?
THE WORTHY THANE OF ROSS!
GOD SAVE THE *KING!*

WHENCE CAM'ST THOU WORTHY THANE?
FROM FIFE, GREAT KING.
-FWUD!
NORWAY HIMSELF, WITH TERRIBLE NUMBERS, ASSISTED BY THAT MOST DISLOYAL TRAITOR THE THANE OF CAWDOR BEGAN A DISMAL CONFLICT.
TILL THAT BELLONA'S BRIDEGROOM, LAPPED IN PROOF, CONFRONTED HIM WITH SELF-COMPARISONS.
ZAP!
FZAP!
POINT AGAINST POINT, REBELLIOUS ARM 'GAINST ARM, CURBING HIS LAVISH SPIRIT, AND TO CONCLUDE...
THE VICTORY FELL ON US.
GREAT HAPPINESS! NO MORE THAT THANE OF CAWDOR SHALL DECEIVE OUR BOSOM INTEREST.
GO PRONOUNCE HIS PRESENT DEATH AND WITH HIS FORMER TITLE GREAT MACBETH.

WHAT HE HATH **LOST**, MACBETH HATH **WON**.
A DRUM, A DRUM MACBETH DOTH COME.
THE WEIRD SISTERS, HAND IN HAND, POSTERS OF THE SEA AND LAND, THUS DO GO ABOUT, THRICE TO THINE, AND THRICE AGAIN, TO MAKE UP NINE, PEACE, THE CHARM'S WOUND UP!
HOW FAR IS IT TO FORRES, MACBETH?
BANQUO, SO FOUL AND FAIR A DAY I HAVE NOT SEEN.
WHAT ARE THESE, SO WITHERED AND SO WILD IN THEIR ATTIRE THAT LOOK NOT LIKE TH' INHABITANTS O' TH' EARTH,
AND YET ARE ON'T?
YOU SHOULD BE WOMEN, AND YET YOUR BEARDS FORBID ME TO INTERPRET THAT YOU ARE SO.

SPEAK IF YOU CAN! WHAT ARE YOU?!
ALL HAIL MACBETH! HAIL TO THEE, THANE OF GLAMIS!
ALL HAIL MACBETH! HAIL TO THEE, THANE OF CAWDOR!
GOOD SIR, WHY DO YOU START AND SEEM TO FEAR THINGS THAT DO SOUND SO FAIR?
IN TH' NAME OF TRUTH, ARE YE FANTASTICAL, OR THAT INDEED WHICH OUTWARDLY YE SHOW? MY NOBLE PARTNER YOU GREET WITH PRESENT GRACE AND OF ROYAL HOPE, THAT HE SEEMS RAPT WITHAL.
TO ME YOU SPEAK NOT.

IF YOU CAN LOOK INTO THE SEEDS OF TIME AND SAY WHICH GRAIN WILL GROW AND WHICH WILL NOT
SPEAK THEN TO ME, WHO NEITHER BEG NOR FEAR YOUR FAVORS NOR YOUR HATE.
!!
?
.
!
!?
NOT SO HAPPY, YET MUCH HAPPIER.
LESSER THAN MACBETH, AND GREATER.
THOU SHALL GET KINGS, THOUGH THOU BE NONE. SO HAIL, *MACBETH* AND *BANQUO!*

STAY, YOU IMPERFECT SPEAKERS, AND TELL ME MORE!
BY FINEL'S DEATH I KNOW I AM THANE OF GLAMIS, BUT HOW OF CAWDOR?
THE THANE OF CAWDOR LIVES, A PROSPEROUS GENTLEMAN. AND TO BE KING STANDS NOT WITHIN THE PROSPECT OR BELIEF, NO MORE THAN TO BE CAWDOR!
SAY FROM WHENCE YOU OWE THIS STRANGE INTELLIGENCE, OR WHY UPON THIS BLASTED HEATH YOU STOP OUR WAY WITH SUCH PROPHETIC GREETING.
SPEAK, I CHARGE YOU.
FWOOSH
THE EARTH HATH BUBBLES AS THE WATER HAS AND THESE ARE THEM.
WHITHER ARE THEY VANISHED?
INTO THE AIR, AND WHAT SEEMED CORPOREAL MELTED AS BREATH INTO THE WIND. WOULD THEY HAVE STAYED!

WERE SUCH THINGS HERE AS WE DO SPEAK ABOUT? OR HAVE WE EATEN ON THE INSANE ROOT THAT TAKES THE REASON PRISONER?
YOUR CHILDREN SHALL BE KINGS.
YOU SHALL BE KING.
AND THANE OF CAWDOR TOO, WHEN IT NOT SO?
TO THE SELFSAME TUNE AND WORDS.
WHO'S HERE?

THE KING HATH HAPPILY RECEIVED, MACBETH, THE NEWS OF THY SUCCESS.
'TIS ROSS
HE BADE ME, FROM HIM, CALL THEE THANE OF CAWDOR, IN WHICH ADDITION, HAIL, MOST WORTHY THANE, FOR IT IS THINE.
WHAT, CAN THE DEVIL SPEAK TRUE?
GLAMIS, AND THANE OF CAWDOR, THE GREATEST IS BEHIND.
TWO TRUTHS ARE TOLD, AS HAPPY PROLOGUES TO THE SWELLING ACT OF THE IMPERIAL THEME.
THIS SUPERNATURAL SOLICITING CANNOT BE ILL, CANNOT BE GOOD. IF ILL, WHY HATH IT GIVEN ME EARNEST OF SUCCESS COMMENCING IN A TRUTH?
PRESENT FEARS ARE LESS THAN HORRIBLE IMAGININGS.
MY THOUGHT, WHOSE MURDER YET IS BUT FANTASTICAL, SHAKES SO MY SINGLE STATE OF MAN THAT FUNCTION IS SMOTHERED IN SURMISE AND NOTHING IS BUT WHAT IS NOT.
IF CHANCE WILL HAVE ME KING, WHY, CHANCE MAY CROWN ME WITHOUT MY STIR.

WORTHY MACBETH, WE STAY UPON YOUR LEISURE.
GIVE ME YOUR FAVOR. MY DULL BRAIN WAS WROUGHT WITH THINGS FORGOTTEN. KIND GENTLEMEN, YOUR PAINS ARE REGISTERED WHERE EVERY DAY I TURN THE LEAF TO READ THEM. LET US TOWARD THE KING.
THINK UPON WHAT HATH CHANCED, AND AT MORE TIME THE INTERIM HAVING WEIGHED IT, LET US SPEAK OUR FREE HEARTS EACH TO OTHER.
VERY GLADLY.
TILL THEN, ENOUGH. *COME FRIENDS!*

O WORTHIEST COUSIN, THE SIN OF MY INGRATITUDE EVEN NOW WAS HEAVY ON ME. THOU ART SO BEFORE THAT SWIFTEST WING OF RECOMPENSE IS SLOW TO OVERTAKE THEE.
THE KING HATH HAPPILY RECEIVED, MACBETH, THE NEWS OF THY SUCCESS.
THE SERVICE AND LOYALTY I OWE, IN DOING IT PAYS ITSELF.
NOBLE BANQUO, LET ME ENFOLD THEE AND HOLD THEE TO MY HEART.
THERE IF I GROW, THE HARVEST IS YOUR OWN.
SONS, KINSMEN, THANES, KNOW WE WILL ESTABLISH OUR ESTATE UPON OUR ELDEST, MALCOLM, WHOM WE NAME HEREAFTER THE PRINCE OF CUMBERLAND, WHICH HONOR MUST.

NOT UNACCOMPANIED INVEST HIM ONLY, BUT SIGNS OF NOBELNESS, LIKE STARS, SHALL SHINE ON ALL DESERVERS. FROM HENCE INVERNESS.
I'LL BE MYSELF THE HARBRINGER, AND MAKE JOYFUL THE HEARING OF MY WIFE WITH YOUR APPROACH, SO, HUMBLY TAKE MY LEAVE.
AND BIND US FURTHER TO YOU.
THE PRINCE OF CUMBERLAND, THAT IS A STEP ON WHICH I MUST FALL DOWN OR ELSE O'ERLEAP, FOR IN MY WAY IT LIES.
STARS, HIDE YOUR FIRES, LET NOT LIGHT SEE MY BLACK AND DEEP DESIRES. THE EYE WINK AT THE HAND, YET LET THAT BE WHICH THE EYE FEARS, WHEN IT IS DONE, TO SEE.

THEY MET ME IN THE DAY OF SUCCESS AND I HAVE LEARNED BY THE PERFECT'ST REPORT THEY HAVE MORE IN THEM THAN MORTAL KNOWLEDGE.
GLAMIS THOU ART, AND CAWDOR, AND SHALT BE WHAT THOU ART PROMISED. YET DO I FEAR THY NATURE.
THESE WEIRD SISTERS SALUTED ME, AND REFFERED ME TO THE COMING ON TIME WITH "HAIL, KING THAT SHALT BE!" THIS HAVE I THOUGHT GOOD TO DELIVER THEE, MY DEAREST PARTNER OF GREATNESS. LAY IT TO THY HEART, AND FAREWELL.
IT IS TOO FULL O' TH' MILK OF HUMAN KINDNESS TO CATCH THE NEAREST WAY. THOU WOULDST BE GREAT, ART NOT WITHOUT AMBITION, BUT WITHOUT...
B-BLEEP!
SERVANT UNIT-7
MESSAGE!
WHAT IS YOUR TIDINGS?
THE KING COMES HERE TONIGHT.
THE RAVEN HIMSELF IS HOARSE THAT CROAKS THE FATAL ENTRANCE OF DUNCAN UNDER MY BATTLEMENTS.
COME, YOU SPIRITS THAT TEND ON MORTAL THOUGHTS, UNSEX ME HERE, AND FILL ME FROM THE CROWN TO THE TOE TOPFUL OF DIREST CRUELTY.

MAKE THICK OF MY *BLOOD!*
STOP UP TH' ACCESS AND PASSAGE TO REMORSE, THAT NO COMPUNCTIONS VISITINGS OF NATURE SHAKE MY FELL PURPOSE NOR KEEP PEACE BETWEEN TH' EFFECT AND IT.
COME TO MY WOMAN'S BREAST AND TAKE OF MY MILK FOR GALL.
COME, THICK NIGHT, AND PALL THEE IN THE DUNNEST SMOKE OF HELL,
THAT IN MY KEEN KNIFE SEE NOT THE WOUND IT MAKES. NOR HEAVEN PEEP THROUGH THE BLANKET OF THE DARK TO CRY "HOLD, HOLD."
GREAT *GLAMIS*, WORTHY *CAWDOR*, GREATER THAN BOTH, BY THE ALL-HAIL HEREAFTER!

THY LETTERS HAVE TRANSPORTED ME BEYOND THIS IGNORANT PRESENT, AND I FEEL NOW THE FUTURE IN THE INSTANT.
MY DEAREST LOVE, KING DUNCAN COMES HERE TONIGHT.
AND WHEN GOES HENCE?
TOMORROW, AS HE PURPOSES.
HO, NEVER SHALL SUN THAT MORROW SEE. YOUR FACE, MY THANE, IS AS A BOOK WHERE MEN MAY READ STRANGE MATTERS. TO BEGUILE THE TIME.
LOOK LIKE THE TIME; BEAR WELCOME IN YOUR EYES, YOUR HAND, YOUR TONGUE. LOOK LIKE TH' INNOCENT FLOWER.

BUT BE THE SERPENT UNDER'T. HE THAT'S COMING MUST BE PROVIDED FOR AND YOU SHALL PUT.
-FUMP
THIS NIGHT'S GREAT BUSINESS INTO MY DISPATCH, WHICH SHALL TO ALL OUR NIGHTS AND DAYS TO COME.
GIVE SOLELY SOVEREIGN SWAY AND MASTERDOM.
WE WILL SPEAK FURTHER.

ONLY LOOK UP CLEAR. TO ALTER FAVOR EVER IS TO FEAR.
LEAVE ALL THE REST TO ME.

THE NEXT DAY, KING DUNCAN AND HIS MEN ARRIVE.
SEE, SEE, OUR HONORED HOSTESS! THE LOVE THAT FOLLOWS US SOMETIME IS OUR TROUBLE, WHICH STILL WE THANK AS LOVE.
HEREIN I TEACH YOU HOW YOU SHALL BID GOD YIELD US FOR YOUR PAINS AND THANK US FOR YOUR TROUBLE.
WHERE'S THE THANE OF CAWDOR? HIS GREAT LOVE, SHARP AS HIS SPUR, HATH HELP HIM TO HIS HOME BEFORE US. FAIR AND NOBLE HOSTESS, WE ARE YOUR GUEST TONIGHT.
ALL OUR SERVICE IN EVERY POINT TWICE DONE, AND THEN DONE DOUBLE, WERE POOR AND SINGLE BUSINESS TO CONTEND AGAINST THOSE HONORS DEEP AND BROAD WHEREWITH YOUR MAJESTY LOAD OUR HOUSE.
GIVE ME YOUR HAND. CONDUCT ME TO MINE HOST, WE LOVE HIM HIGHLY AND SHALL CONTINUE OUR GRACES TOWARDS HIM.

IF IT WERE DONE WHEN 'TIS DONE, THEN 'TWERE WELL IT WERE DONE QUICKLY. BUT THIS BLOW MIGHT BE THE BE-ALL AND THE END-ALL.
HERE BUT UPON THIS BAND AND SHOAL OF TIME WE'D JUMP THE LIFE TO COME.
BUT IN THESE CASES WE STILL HAVE THE JUDGEMENT HERE, THAT WE BIT TEACH BLOODY INSTRUCTION, WHICH, BEING TAUGHT, RETURN TO PLAGUE TH' INVENTOR. THIS EVENHANDED JUSTICE COMMENDS TH' INGREDIENCE OF OUR POISONED CHALICE TO OUR OWN LIPS.
HE'S HERE IN DOUBLE TRUST, FIRST AS I AM HIS KINSMAN AND HIS SUBJECT, STRONG BOTH AGAINST THE DEED, THEN, AS HIS HOST.
WHO SHOULD AGAINST HIS MURDERER SHUT THE DOOR, NOR BEAR THE KNIFE MYSELF. BESIDES, HIS VIRTUES WILL PLEAD LIKE ANGLES, TRUMPET-TONGUED AGAINST THE DEEP DAMNATION OF HIS TAKING-OFF.
I HAVE NO SPUR TO PRICK THE SIDES OF MY INTENT, BUT ONLY VAULTING AMBITION, WHICH O'ERLEAPS ITSELFT AND FALLS ON TH' OTHER.

!?
HE HAS ALMOST SUPPED. WHY HAVE YOU LEFT THE CHAMBER?
HATH HE ASKED FOR ME?
KNOW YOU NOT HE HAS?
WE WILL PROCEED NO FURTHER IN THIS BUSINESS. HE HATH HONORED ME OF LATE, AND I HAVE BOUGHT GOLDEN OPINIONS FROM ALL SORTS OF PEOPLE.
WHICH WOULD BE WORN NOW IN THEIR NEWEST GLOSS, NOT CAST ASIDE SO SOON.
WAS THE HOPE DRUNK WHEREIN YOU DRESSED YOURSELF? HATH IT SLEPT SINCE?
AND WAKES IT NOW TO LOOK SO GREEN AND PALE AT WHAT IT DID SO FREELY?
FROM THIS TIME SUCH I ACCOUNT THY LOVE.

ART THOU AFEARED TO BE THE SAME IN THINE OWN ACT AND VALOR AS THOU ART IN DESIRE?
WOULDST THOU HAVE THAT WHICH THOU ESTEEM'ST THE ORNAMENT OF LIFE AND A COWARD IN THINE OWN ESTEEM, LETTING "I DARE NOT" WAIT UPON "I WOULD."
PRITHEE PEACE, I DARE DO ALL THAT MAY BECOME A MAN, WHO DARES DO MORE IS NONE.
WHAT BEAST WAS'T THEN THAT MADE YOU BREAK THIS ENTERPRISE TO ME? WHEN YOU DURST DO IT, THEN YOU WERE A MAN, AND TO BE MORE THAN WHAT YOU WERE, YOU WOULD BE MORE THE MAN.
NOR TIME NOR PLACE DID THEN ADHERE, AND YET YOU WOULD MAKE BOTH. THEY HAVE MADE THEMSELVES, AND THAT THEIR FITNESS NOW DOES UNMAKE YOU.

IF WE SHOULD FAIL?
WE FAIL?
BUT SCREW YOUR COURAGE TO THE STICKING PLACE AND WE'LL NOT FAIL. WHEN DUNCAN IS ASLEEP, WHERETO THE RATHER SHALL HIS DAY'S HARD JOURNEY SOUNDLY INVITE HIM.
HIS TWO CHAMBERLAINS WILL I WITH WINE AND WASSAIL SO CONVINCE THAT MEMORY, THE WARDER OF THE BRAIN, SHALL BE A FUME, AND THE RECEIPT OF REASON A LIMBICK ONLY.
WHEN IN SWINISH SLEEP THEIR DRENCHED NATURE LIES AS IN A DEATH, WHAT CANNOT YOU AND I PERFORM UPON TH' UNGUARDED DUNCAN?

WHAT NOT PUT UPON HIS SPONGY OFFICERS, WHO SHALL BEAR THE GUILT OF GREAT QUELL?
BRING FORTH MEN-CHILDREN ONLY, FOR THY UNDAUNTED METTLE SHOULD COMPOSE NOTHING BUT MALES. WILL IT NOT BE RECEIVED WHEN WE HAVE MARKED WITH BLOOD THOSE SLEEPY TWO OF HIS OWN CHAMBER?
WHO DARES RECEIVE IT OTHER, AS WE SHALL MAKE OUR GRIEFS AND CLAMOR ROAR UPON HIS DEATH?

I AM SETTLED, AND BEND UP EACH CORPOREAL AGENT TO THIS TERRIBLE FEAT. AWAY, AND MOCK THE TIME WITH FAIREST SHOW.
FALSE FACE MUST HIDE WHAT THE FALSE HEART DOTH KNOW.

JUST AFTER MIDNIGHT...
FLEANCE, A HEAVY SUMMONS LIES LIKE LEAD UPON ME, AND YET I WOULD NOT SLEEP.
WHO'S THERE?
A FRIEND, BANQUO.
THE KING'S ABED. HE HATH BEEN IN UNUSUAL PLEASURE AND SENT FORTH GREAT LARGESS TO YOUR OFFICES.
THIS DIAMOND HE GREETS YOUR WIFE WITHAL BY THE NAME OF MOST KIND HOSTESS.

I DREAMT LAST NIGHT OF THE THREE WEIRD SISTERS. TO YOU THEY HAVE SHOWED SOME TRUTH.
I THINK NOT OF THEM. YET WHEN WE CAN ENTREAT AN HOUR TO SERVE...
WE WOULD SPEND IT IN SOME WORDS UPON THAT BUSINESS, IF YOU WOULD GRANT THE TIME.
AT YOUR KIND'ST LEISURE.
IS THIS A DAGGER WHICH I SEE BEFORE ME, THE HANDLE TOWARD MY HAND? COME, LET ME CLUTCH THEE.

I HAVE THEE NOT, AND YET I SEE THEE STILL. ART THOU NOT, FATAL VISION, SENSIBLE TO FEELING AS TO SIGHT?
OR ART THOU BUT A DAGGER OF THE MIND, A FALSE CREATION PROCEEDING FROM THE HEAT-OPPRESSED BRAIN?
I SEE THEE YET, IN FORM AS PALPABLE AS THIS WHICH I NOW DRAW.
KLINK!
I GO, AND IT IS DONE. THE BELL INVITES ME. HEAR IT NOT, DUNCAN, FOR IT IS A KNELL THAT SUMMONS THEE TO HEAVEN, OR TO HELL.

ZZZZ...

THAT WHICH HATH MADE THEM DRUNK HATH MADE ME BOLD, WHAT HATH QUENCHED THEM HATH GIVEN ME FIRE.
KRAAWK!!
HARK! PEACE.
THE DOORS ARE OPEN.
I HAVE DRUGGED THEIR POSSETS THAT DEATH AND NATURE DO CONTEND ABOUT THEM WHETHER THEY LIVE OR DIE.

?!
WHO'S THERE? WHAT, HO?
ALACK, I AM AFRAID THEY HAVE AWAKED, AND 'TIS NOT DONE. TH' ATTEMPT, AND NOT THE DEED, CONFOUNDS US. HARK!
I LAID THEIR DAGGERS READY, HE COULD NOT MISS 'EM.
HAD HE NOT RESEMBLED MY FATHER AS HE SLEPT, I HAD DONE'T.

MY HUSBAND!
I HAVE DONE THE DEED.
DIDST THOU NOT HEAR A NOISE?
I HEARD THE OWL SCREAM AND THE CRICKETS CRY. DID NOT YOU SPEAK?
WHEN?
NOW.
AS I DESCENDED?
AY.

METHOUGHT I HEARD A VOICE CRY "SLEEP NO MORE! MACBETH DOTH MURDER SLEEP."
WHAT DO YOU MEAN?
STILL IT CRIED "SLEEP NO MORE!" TO ALL THE HOUSE.
"GLAMIS HATH MURDERED SLEEP, AND THEREFORE CAWDOR SHALL SLEEP NO MORE, MACBETH SHALL SLEEP NO MORE."
WHO WAS IT THAT THUS CRIED? WHY, WORTHY THANE, YOU DO UNBEND YOUR NOBLE STRENGTH TO THINK SO BRAINSICKLY OF THINGS.
GO GET SOME WATER AND WASH THIS FILTHY WITNESS FROM YOUR HAND.

WHY DID YOU BRING THE DAGGERS FROM THE PLACE? THEY MUST LIE THERE. GO CARRY THEM AND SMEAR THE SLEEPY GROOMS WITH BLOOD.
I'LL GO NO MORE. I AM AFRAID TO THINK WHAT I HAVE DONE.
LOOK ON'T AGAIN I DARE NOT.
FWIP!
SNATCH!!
INFIRM OF PURPOSE! GIVE ME THE DAGGERS.
IF HE DO BLEED I'LL GILD THE FACES OF THE GROOMS WITHAL, FOR IT MUST SEEM THEIR GUILT.

WHENCE IS THAT KNOCKING? HOW IS'T WITH ME WHEN EVERY NOISE APPALLS ME? WHAT HANDS ARE HERE? HA! THEY PLUCK OUT MINE EYES.

WILL ALL GREAT NEPTUNE'S OCEAN WASH THIS BLOOD CLEAN FROM MY HAND?
NO, THIS MY HAND WILL RATHER THE MULTITUDINOUS SEAS INCARNADINE, MAKING THE GREEN ONE RED.
MY HANDS ARE OF YOUR COLOR, BUT I SHAME TO WEAR A HEART SO WHITE.
I HEAR A KNOCKING. RETIRE WE TO OUR CHAMBER, A LITTLE WATER CLEARS US OF THIS DEED.
GET ON YOUR NIGHTGOWN, LEST OCCASION CALL US AND SHOW US TO BE WATCHERS.

TO KNOW MY DEED, TWERE BEST NOT KNOW MYSELF.
NOK NOK
WAKE DUNCAN WITH THY KNOCKING, I WOULD THOU COULDST.
NOK NOK
HERE'S A KNOCKING INDEED.
OUR KNOCKING HAS AWAKED HIM, HERE HE COMES.
IS THY MASTER STIRRING?

GOOD MORROW, NOBLE MACBETH.
IS THE KING STIRRING, WORTHY THANE?
MACBETH, LENNOX, GOOD MORROW, BOTH.
NOT YET, MACDUFF.
HE DID COMMAND ME TO CALL TIMELY ON HIM, I HAVE ALMOST SLIPPED THE HOUR.
I'LL MAKE SO BOLD TO CALL, FOR 'TIS MY LIMITED SERVICE.
I'LL BRING YOU TO HIM.
THE NIGHT HAS BEEN UNRULY.

SOME SAY THE EARTH WAS FEVEROUS AND DID SHAKE.
'TWAS A ROUGH NIGHT.
O HORROR, HORROR, HORROR! CONFUSION NOW HATH MADE HIS MASTERPIECE!
MOST SACRILEGIOUS MURDER HATH BROKE OPEN!
APPROACH THE CHAMBER. DO NOT BID ME SPEAK. SEE, AND THEN SPEAK YOURSELVES.

BANQUO AND DONALBAIN! MALCOLM, AWAKE! SHAKE OFF THIS DOWNY SLEEP, DEATH'S COUNTERFEIT!
...
?!
MALCOLM! BANQUO! AS FROM YOUR GRAVES RISE UP AND WALK LIKE SPRITES!
AND COUNTENANCE THIS HORROR.

WHAT'S THE BUSINESS? SPEAK!
O GENTLE LADY...
'TIS NOT FOR TO HEAR WHAT I CAN SPEAK, THE REPETITION IN A WOMAN'S EAR WOULD MURDER AS IT FELL.
O BANQUO, BANQUO, OUR ROYAL MASTER'S MURDERED!
WOE, ALAS!
WHAT, IN OUR HOUSE?
FLASH!

TOO CRUEL ANYWHERE. DEAR DUFF, SAY IT IS NOT SO.
RENOWN AND GRACE IS DEAD, THE WINE OF LIFE IS DRAWN, AND THE MERE LEES IS LEFT THIS VAULT TO BRAG OF.
WHAT IS AMISS?
MALCOLM, DONALBAIN, THE SPRING, THE HEAD, THE FOUNTAIN OF YOUR BLOOD IS STOPPED.

YOUR ROYAL FATHER'S MURDERED.
O, BY WHOM?!
THOSE OF HIS CHAMBER... NO MAN'S LIFE WAS TO BE TRUSTED WITH THEM.
O, YET I DO REPENT THAT I DID KILL THEM.
WHEREFORE DID YOU SO?!

WHO COULD REFRAIN THAT HAD A HEART TO LOVE, AND IN THAT HEART COURAGE TO MAKE LOVE KNOWN?
HELP ME HENCE, HO!
LOOK TO THE LADY.
DONALBAIN, WHY DO WE HOLD OUR TONGUES THAT MOST MAY CLAIM THIS ARGUMENT FOR OURS?
WHAT SHOULD BE SPOKEN HERE, MALCOLM.

LET'S AWAY; OUR TEARS ARE NOT YET BREWED.
NOR OUR STRONG SORROW UPON THE FOOT OF MOTION.
SEE TO LADY MACBETH.
WHAT NOW, BANQUO?
LET US MEET AND QUESTION THIS MOST BLOODY PIECE OF WORK, TO KNOW IT FURTHER.
AGAINST THE UNDIVULGED PRETENSE I FIGHT OF TREASONOUS MALICE. WHAT SAY YOU, MACDUFF?
AND SO DO I.

WHAT WILL YOU DO? LET'S NOT CONSORT WITH THEM. TO SHOW AN UNFELT SORROW IS AN OFFICE WHICH THE FALSE MAN DOES EASY.
I'LL TO ENGLAND.
TO IRELAND I.
THEREFORE TO HORSE!
AND LET US NOT BE DAINTY OF LEAVE-TAKING...

"BUT SHIFT AWAY. THERE'S WARRANT IN THAT THEFT WHICH STEALS ITSELF WHEN THERE'S NO MERCY LEFT."
THREESCORE AND TEN I CAN REMEMBER WELL...
...WITHIN THE VOLUME OF WHICH TIME I HAVE SEEN HOURS DREADFUL AND THINGS STRANGE...
...BUT THIS SORE NIGHT HATH TRIFLED FORMER KNOWINGS.

'TIS UNNATURAL, ROSS.
ON TUESDAY LAST A FALCON...
AND DUNCAN'S HORSES...
...WAS BY A MOUSING OWL HAWKED AT AND KILLED.
"...BROKE THEIR STALLS, FLUNG OUT CONTENDING 'GAINST OBEDIENCE."
'TIS SAID THEY ATE EACH OTHER.
"THEY DID SO, TO TH' AMAZEMENT OF MINE EYES."

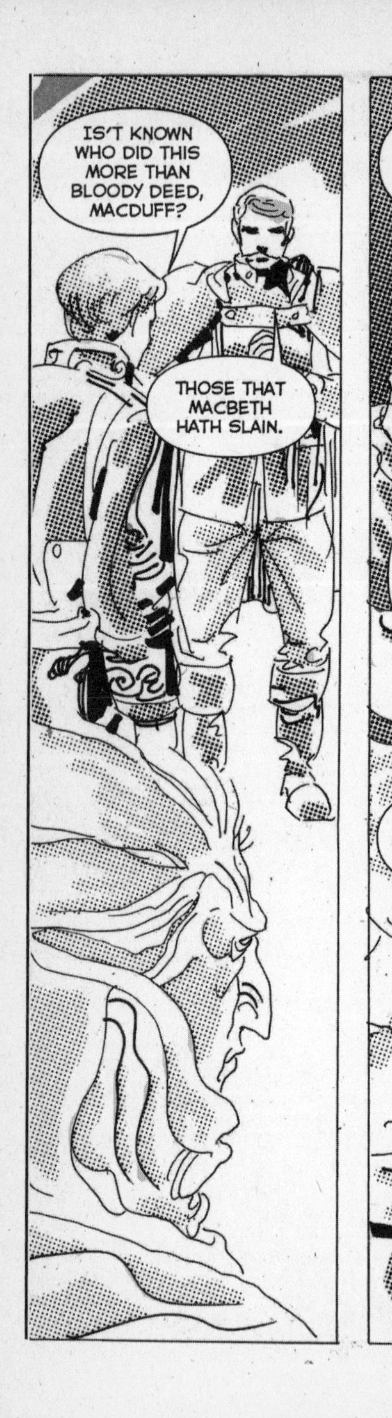
IS'T KNOWN WHO DID THIS MORE THAN BLOODY DEED, MACDUFF?
THOSE THAT MACBETH HATH SLAIN.

MALCOLM AND DONALBAIN, THE KING'S TWO SONS...
...ARE STOL'N AWAY AND FLED, WHICH PUTS UPON THEM SUSPICION OF THE DEED.
THEN...THE SOVEREIGNTY WILL FALL UPON MACBETH.
HE IS ALREADY NAMED, AND GONE TO SCONE TO BE INVESTED, ROSS.
WILL YOU TO SCONE, MACDUFF?
NO, COUSIN, I'LL TO FIFE.
WELL, I WILL THITHER.

FAREWELL, FATHER.
GOD'S BENISON GO WITH YOU, AND WITH THOSE THAT WOULD MAKE GOOD OF BAD, AND FRIENDS OF FOES.
THOU HAST IT NOW, KING, CAWDOR, GLAMIS, ALL AS THE WEIRD WOMEN PROMISED...AND I FEAR THOU PLAYED MOST FOULLY FOR IT.

MY LORD MACBETH.
HERE'S OUR CHIEF GUEST, BANQUO.

MY DUTIES ARE WITH A MOST INDISSOLUBLE TIE...
...FOREVER KNIT.

RIDE YOU THIS AFTERNOON?
AY, MY GOOD LORD.
IS'T FAR YOU RIDE?
AS FAR, MY LORD, AS WILL FILL UP THE TIME BETWEEN THIS AND SUPPER.
FAIL NOT OUR FEAST.
I WILL NOT, M'LORD MACBETH.
WE HEAR OUR BLOODY COUSINS ARE IN ENGLAND AND IN IRELAND.

BUT OF THAT TOMORROW. HIE YOU TO HORSE.
AY, MY GOOD LORD. OUR TIME DOES CALL UPON US.
FAREWELL.
LET EVERY MAN BE MASTER OF HIS TIME...GOD BE WITH YOU.
SIRRAH, A WORD WITH YOU.

ATTEND THOSE MEN OUR PLEASURE?
THEY ARE, MY LORD, WITHOUT THE PALACE GATE.
BRING THEM BEFORE US.
OUR FEARS IN BANQUO STICK DEEP AND IN HIS ROYALTRY OF NATURE REIGNS THAT WHICH WOULD BE FEARED.
THE SISTERS HAILED HIM FATHER TO A LINE OF KINGS.
UPON MY HEAD THEY PLACED A FRUITLESS CROWN AND PUT A BARREN SCEPTER IN MY GRIP...

THENCE TO BE WRENCHED WITH AN UNLINEAL HAND, NO SON OF MY MINE SUCCEEDING.
FOR BANQUO'S ISSUE THE GRACIOUS DUNCAN HAVE I MURDERED...
WHO'S THERE?

NOW GO TO THE DOOR AND STAY THERE TILL WE CALL.
WAS IT NOT YESTERDAY WE SPOKE TOGETHER?
IT WAS, SO PLEASE MILORD MACBETH.
WELL THEN NOW HAVE YOU CONSIDERED OF MY SPEECHES?
KNOW THAT IT WAS HE WHO HELD YOU SO UNDER FORTUNE... CROSSED...

ARE YOU SO GOSPELL'D TO PRAY FOR THIS GOOD MAN...WHOSE HEAVY HAND BOWED YOU TO THE GRAVE...?
AY, IN THE CATALOGUE YE GO FOR MEN, AS HOUNDS... MONGRELS... CURS...AND DEMIWOLVES...
...ALL BY THE NAME OF DOGS.
NOW IF YOU HAVE A STATION IN THE FILE, NOT IN THE WORST RANK OF MANHOOD,SAY IT.

I WILL PUT THAT BUSINESS IN YOUR BOSOMS WHOSE EXECUTION TAKES YOUR ENEMY OFF...
THE VILE BLOWS AND BUFFETS OF THE WORLD HAVE SO INCENSED ME THAT...
...I WOULD SET MY LIFE ON MY CHANCE TO MEND IT OR BE RID ON'T.
BOTH OF YOU KNOW BANQUO WAS YOUR ENEMY.
TRUE, MY LORD.
SO IS HE MINE...AND THOUGH I COULD WITH BAREFACED POWER SWEEP FROM MY SIGHT AND BID MY WILL AVOUCH FOR IT...

YET I MUST NOT... AND THENCE IT IS THAT I TO YOUR ASSISTANCE DO MAKE LOVE...

MASKING THE BUSINESS FROM THE COMMON EYE FOR SUNDRY WEIGHTY REASONS.
WE SHALL, MY LORD, PERFORM WHAT YOU COMMAND US.
THOUGH OUR LIVES...

YOUR SPIRITS SHINE THROUGH YOU. WITHIN THIS HOUR AT MOST I WILL ADVISE YOU WHERE TO PLANT YOURSELVES...

TO LEAVE NO RUBS NOR BOTCHES IN THE WORK, FLEANCE HIS SON...MUST EMBRACE THE FATE OF THAT DARK HOUR. RESOLVE YOURSELF...
WE ARE RESOLVED, MY LORD.
IT IS CONCLUDED. BANQUO, THY SOUL'S FLIGHT, IF IT FIND HEAVEN, MUST FIND IT OUT TONIGHT.

IS BANQUO GONE FROM COURT?
AY, MADAM, BUT RETURNS AGAIN TONIGHT.
SAY TO THE KING I WOULD ATTEND HIS LEISURE FOR A FEW WORDS.
MADAM, I WILL.
NAUGHT'S HAD, ALL'S SPENT, WHERE OUR DESIRE IS GOT WITHOUT CONTENT.
'TIS SAFER TO BE THAT WHICH WE DESTROY THAN BY DESTRUCTION DWELL IN DOUBTFUL JOY.

HOW NOW, MY LORD? WHY DO YOU KEEP ALONE? ...WHAT'S DONE IS DONE.
WE HAVE SCORCHED THE SNAKE, NOT KILLED IT.
BETTER BE WITH THE DEAD.... DUNCAN IS IN HIS GRAVE; AFTER LIFE'S FITFUL FEVER HE SLEEPS WELL.
O, FULL OF SCORPIONS IS MY MIND, DEAR WIFE THOU KNOW'ST THAT BANQUO, AND HIS FLEANCE, LIVES

BUT IN THEM NATURE'S COPY'S NOT ETERNE.
THERE'S COMFORT YET, THEY ARE ASSAILABLE... ERE THE BAT HATH FLOWN... THERE SHALL BE DONE A DEED OF DREADFUL NOTE.
WHAT'S TO BE DONE?
BE INNOCENT OF THE KNOWLEDGE, DEAREST CHUCK, TILL THOU APPLAUD THE DEED.
COME, SEELING NIGHT... AND TEAR TO PIECES THAT GREAT BOND WHICH KEEPS ME PALE.
GOOD THINGS OF DAY BEGIN TO DROOP AND DROWSE.

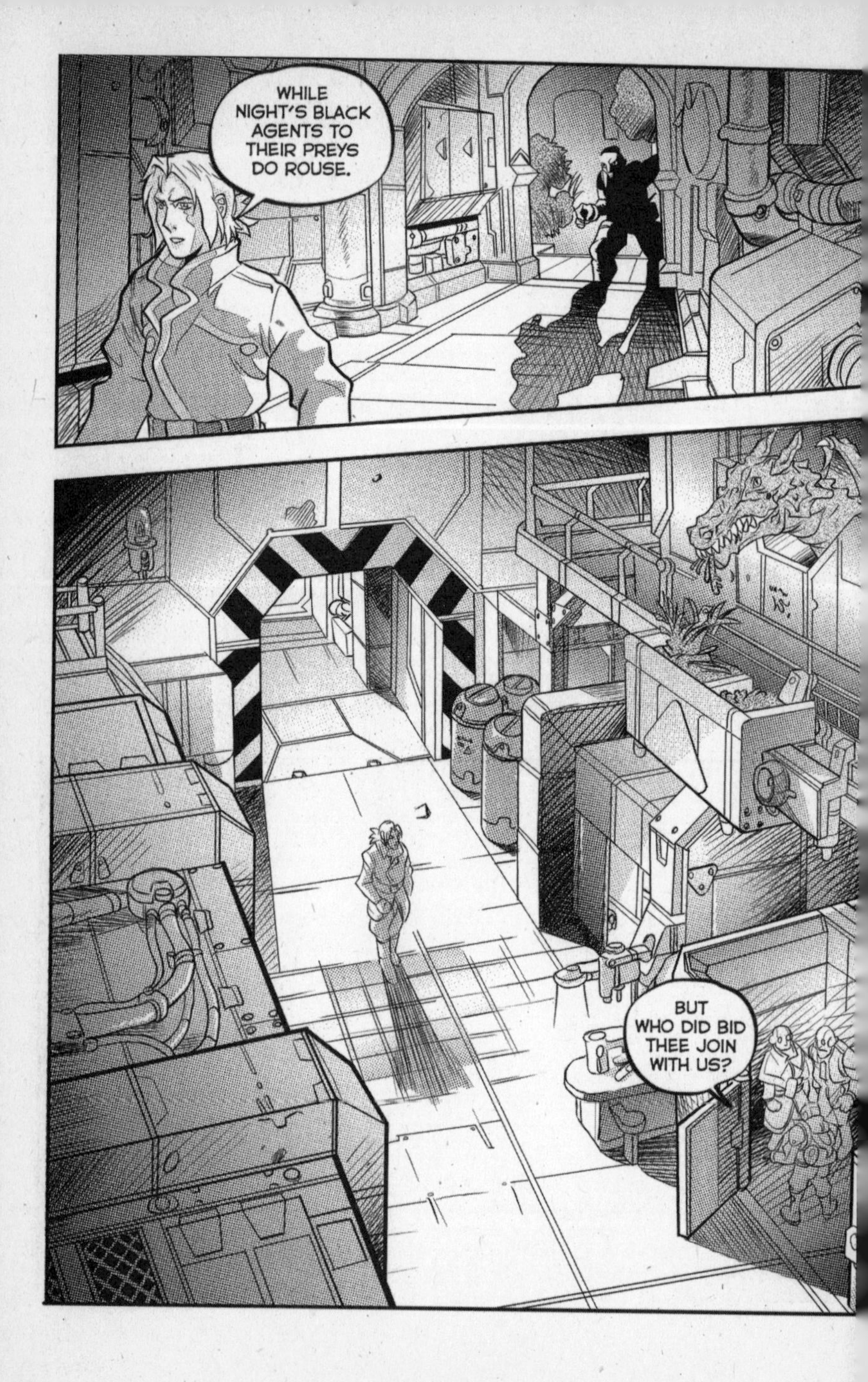
WHILE NIGHT'S BLACK AGENTS TO THEIR PREYS DO ROUSE.
BUT WHO DID BID THEE JOIN WITH US?

MACBETH.
HE NEEDS NOT OUR MISTRUST, SINCE HE DELIVERS OUR OFFICES AND WHAT WE HAVE TO DO TO THE DIRECTIONS JUST.
THEN STAND WITH US.
HARK, I HEAR HORSES.
GIVE US A LIGHT THERE, HO!

THEN 'TIS HE, BANQUO, THE REST THAT ARE WITHIN THE NOTE OF EXPECTATION ALREADY ARE IN THE COURT.
HIS HORSES GO ABOUT.
ALMOST A MILE, BUT HE DOES USUALLY, SO ALL MEN DO, FROM HENCE TO THE PALACE GATE MAKE IT THEIR WALK.
IT WILL BE RAIN TONIGHT.

ZAP!
LET IT COME DOWN!
FZAP!
O, TREACHERY!
FWASH!
SNIK!

FLY,
GOOD FLEANCE,
FLY, *FLY*,
FLY!
THOU
MAYEST
REVENGE,
O SLAVE!
WHOOSH..

THERE'S BUT ONE DOWN, THE SON IS FLED.
WE HAVE LOST BEST HALF OF OUR AFFAIR.
WELL, LET'S AWAY, AND SAY HOW MUCH IS DONE.

MEANWHILE, AT THE BANQUET HOSTED BY MACBETH...
BE LARGE IN MIRTH; ANON WE'LL DRINK A MEASURE THE TABLE ROUND.
THERE'S BLOOD UPON THY FACE.
'TIS BANQUO'S THEN.

'TIS BETTER THEE WITHOUT THAN HE WITHIN.
MY LORD, HIS THROAT IS CUT; THAT I DID FOR HIM.
THOU ART THE BEST O' TH' CUTTHROATS. YET HE'S GOOD THAT DID THE LIKE FOR FLEANCE.
MOST ROYAL SIR, FLEANCE IS ESCAPED.
THEN COMES MY FIT AGAIN.

NOW I AM CABINED, CRIBBED, CONFINED, BOUND IN TO SAUCY DOUBTS AND FEARS.

BUT BANQUO'S SAFE?
AY, MY GOOD LORD. SAFE IN A DITCH HE HIDES, WITH TWENTY TRENCHED GASHES ON HIS HEAD, THE LEAST A DEATH TO NATURE.

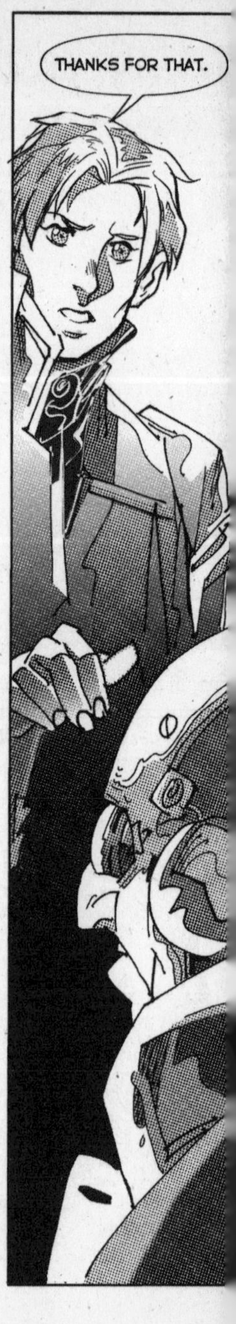
THANKS FOR THAT.

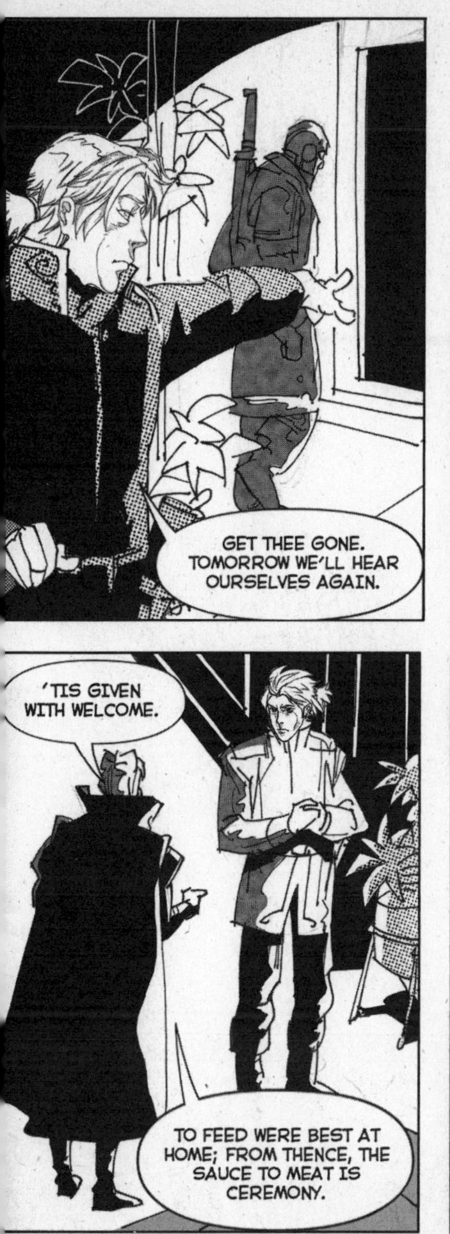
GET THEE GONE. TOMORROW WE'LL HEAR OURSELVES AGAIN.
'TIS GIVEN WITH WELCOME.
TO FEED WERE BEST AT HOME; FROM THENCE, THE SAUCE TO MEAT IS CEREMONY.

MY ROYAL LORD, YOU DO NOT GIVE THE CHEER.
THE FEAST IS SOLD THAT IS NOT OFTEN VOUCHED, WHILE 'T IS A-MAKING.

MEETING WERE BARE WITHOUT IT.

SWEET REMEMBRANCE! NOW GOOD DIGESTION WAIT ON APPETITE, AND HEALTH ON BOTH.
MAY'T PLEASE YOUR HIGHNESS, SIT.
HERE HAD WE NOW OUR COUNTRY'S HONOR ROOFED WERE THE GRACED PERSON OF...
...OUR...BANQUO... PRESENT...

WHO MAY I RATHER... CHALLENGE FOR... UNKINDNESS...THAN PITY FOR MISCHANCE.
BANQUO'S GHOST!
HIS ABSENCE, SIR, LAYS BLAME UPON HIS PROMISE. PLEASE'T YOUR HIGHNESS TO GRACE US WITH YOUR ROYAL COMPANY.
THE...TABLE'S FULL.
HERE IS A PLACE RESERVED, SIR.
WHERE?
THIS EMPTY THRONE, MY GOOD LORD. WHAT IS'T THAT MOVES YOUR HIGH-NESS?

WHICH OF YOU HAVE DONE THIS?
WHAT, MY GOOD LORD?
THOU CANST NOT SAY I DID IT. NEVER SHAKE THY GORY LOCKS AT ME.
GENTLEMEN, RISE. HIS HIGH-NESS IS NOT WELL.
SIT, WORTHY FRIENDS. MY LORD IS OFTEN THUS, AND HATH BEEN FROM HIS YOUTH. PRAY YOU KEEP SEAT.

THE FIT IS MOMENTARY; UPON A THOUGHT HE WILL AGAIN BE WELL. FEED, AND REGARD HIM NOT.
ARE YOU A MAN?
AY, AND A BOLD ONE, THAT DARE LOOK ON THAT WHICH MIGHT APPALL THE DEVIL.
O PROPER STUFF! THIS IS THE VERY PAINTING OF YOUR FEAR.
THIS IS THE AIR-DRAWN DAGGER WHICH YOU SAID LED YOU TO DUNCAN.

SHAME ITSELF! WHY DO YOU MAKE SUCH FACES?
WHEN ALL'S DONE, YOU LOOK BUT ON A STOOL.
PRITHEE SEE THERE! BEHOLD! LOOK! LO!
HOW SAY YOU? WHY, WHAT CARE I? IF THOU CANST NOD, SPEAK TOO.

IF CHARNEL HOUSES AND OUR GRAVES MUST SEND THOSE THAT WE BURY BACK, OUR MONUMENTS SHALL BE THE MAWS OF KITES.
WHAT, QUITE UNMANNED IN FOLLY?
IF I STAND HERE, I SAW HIM.
FIE, FOR SHAME!
THE TIME HAS BEEN THAT ...THE MAN WOULD DIE, AND THERE WAS AN END.

BUT NOW THEY RISE AGAIN...AND PUSH US FROM OUR STOOLS. THIS IS MORE STRANGE THAN SUCH A MURDER IS.

MY WORTHY LORD, YOUR NOBLE FRIENDS DO LACK YOU.
I DO FORGET. DO NOT MUSE AT ME, MY MOST WORTHY FRIENDS.

I HAVE A STRANGE INFIRMITY, WHICH IS NOTHING TO THOSE THAT KNOW ME.

COME, LOVE AND HEALTH TO ALL, THEN I'LL SIT DOWN. I DRINK TO THE GENERAL JOY OF THE WHOLE TABLE.

AND TO OUR DEAR FRIEND BANQUO, WHOM WE MISS. WOULD HE WERE HERE!
TO ALL, AND HIM WE THIRST, AND ALL TO ALL.
OUR DUTIES, AND THE PLEDGE.

GAKK
WHAT MAN DARE, I DARE...TAKE ANY SHAPE BUT THAT, AND MY FIRM NERVES SHALL NEVER TREMBLE.
AVAUNT, AND QUIT MY SIGHT! LET THE EARTH HIDE THEE!
THINK OF THIS, GOOD PEERS, BUT AS A THING OF CUSTOM. ONLY IT SPOILS THE PLEA-SURE OF THE TIME.

OR BE ALIVE AGAIN, AND DARE ME TO THE DESERT WITH THY SWORD...HENCE, HOR-RIBLE SHADOW! UNREAL MOCK'RY, HENCE!
WHY, SO; BEING GONE, I AM A MAN AGAIN. PRAY YOU SIT STILL.
YOU HAVE DISPLACED THE MIRTH, BROKE THE GOOD MEETING WITH MOST ADMIRED DISORDER.
YOU MAKE ME STRANGE EVEN TO THE DISPOSITION THAT I OWE.

WHEN NOW I THINK YOU CAN BEHOLD SUCH SIGHTS AND KEEP THE NATURAL RUBY OF YOUR CHEEKS WHEN MINE IS BLANCHED WITH FEAR.
WHAT SIGHTS, MY LORD?
I PRAY YOU SPEAK NOT; QUESTION ENRAGES HIM.
STAND NOT UPON THE ORDER OF YOUR GOING, BUT GO AT ONCE.
GOOD NIGHT AND BETTER HEALTH.
A KIND GOOD NIGHT TO ALL.

IT WILL HAVE BLOOD, THEY SAY; BLOOD WILL HAVE BLOOD...

ALMOST AT ODDS WITH MORNING, WHICH IS WHICH.
HOW SAY'ST THOU, THAT MACDUFF DENIES HIS PERSON AT OUR BIDDING?
DID YOU SEND TO HIM, SIR?
I HEAR IT BY THE WAY; BUT I WILL SEND. I WILL TOMORROW, AND BETIMES I WILL TO THE WEIRD SISTERS.

MORE SHALL THEY SPEAK...
...FOR NOW I AM BENT TO KNOW BY THE WORST MEANS THE WORST.
STRANGE THINGS I HAVE IN HEAD, THAT WILL TO HAND...
...WHICH MUST BE ACTED ERE THEY MAY BE SCANNED.
YOU LACK THE SEASON OF ALL NATURES, SLEEP.
COME, WE'LL TO SLEEP.
MY STRANGE AND SELF-ABUSE IS THE INITIATE FEAR THAT WANTS HARD USE.
WE ARE YET BUT YOUNG IN DEED.

WHY, HOW NOW,
HECATE? YOU
LOOK ANGERLY.

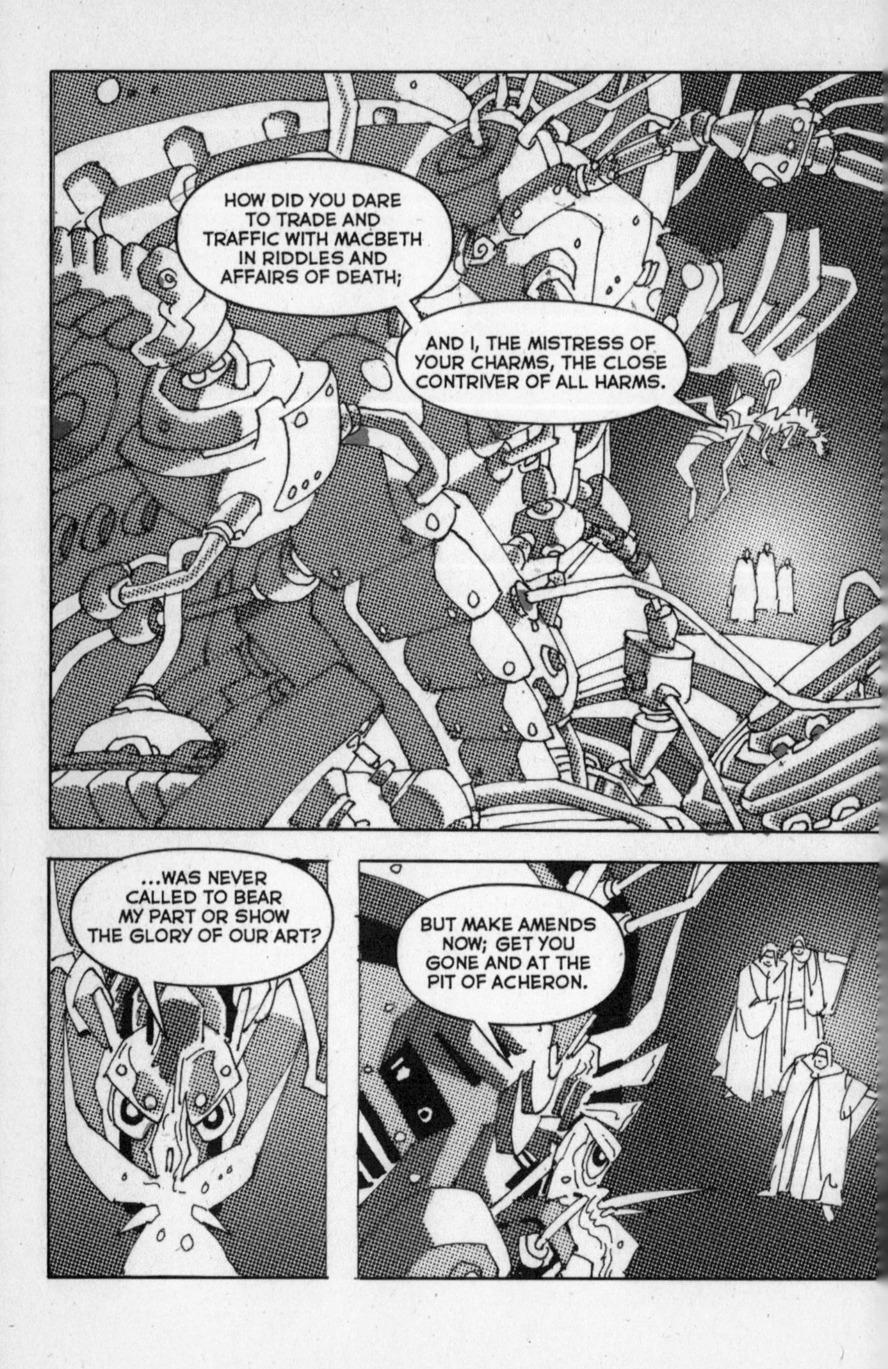
HOW DID YOU DARE TO TRADE AND TRAFFIC WITH MACBETH IN RIDDLES AND AFFAIRS OF DEATH;
AND I, THE MISTRESS OF YOUR CHARMS, THE CLOSE CONTRIVER OF ALL HARMS.
...WAS NEVER CALLED TO BEAR MY PART OR SHOW THE GLORY OF OUR ART?
BUT MAKE AMENDS NOW; GET YOU GONE AND AT THE PIT OF ACHERON.

MEET ME IN THE MORNING. THITHER HE WILL COME TO KNOW HIS DESTINY.
YOUR VESSELS AND YOUR SPELLS PRO-VIDE...
...YOUR CHARMS AND EVERYTHING.
GREAT BUSINESS MUST BE WROUGHT ERE NOON...
THERE HANGS A VAPOROUS DROP PROFOUND I'LL CATCH IT ERE IT COMES TO GROUND...

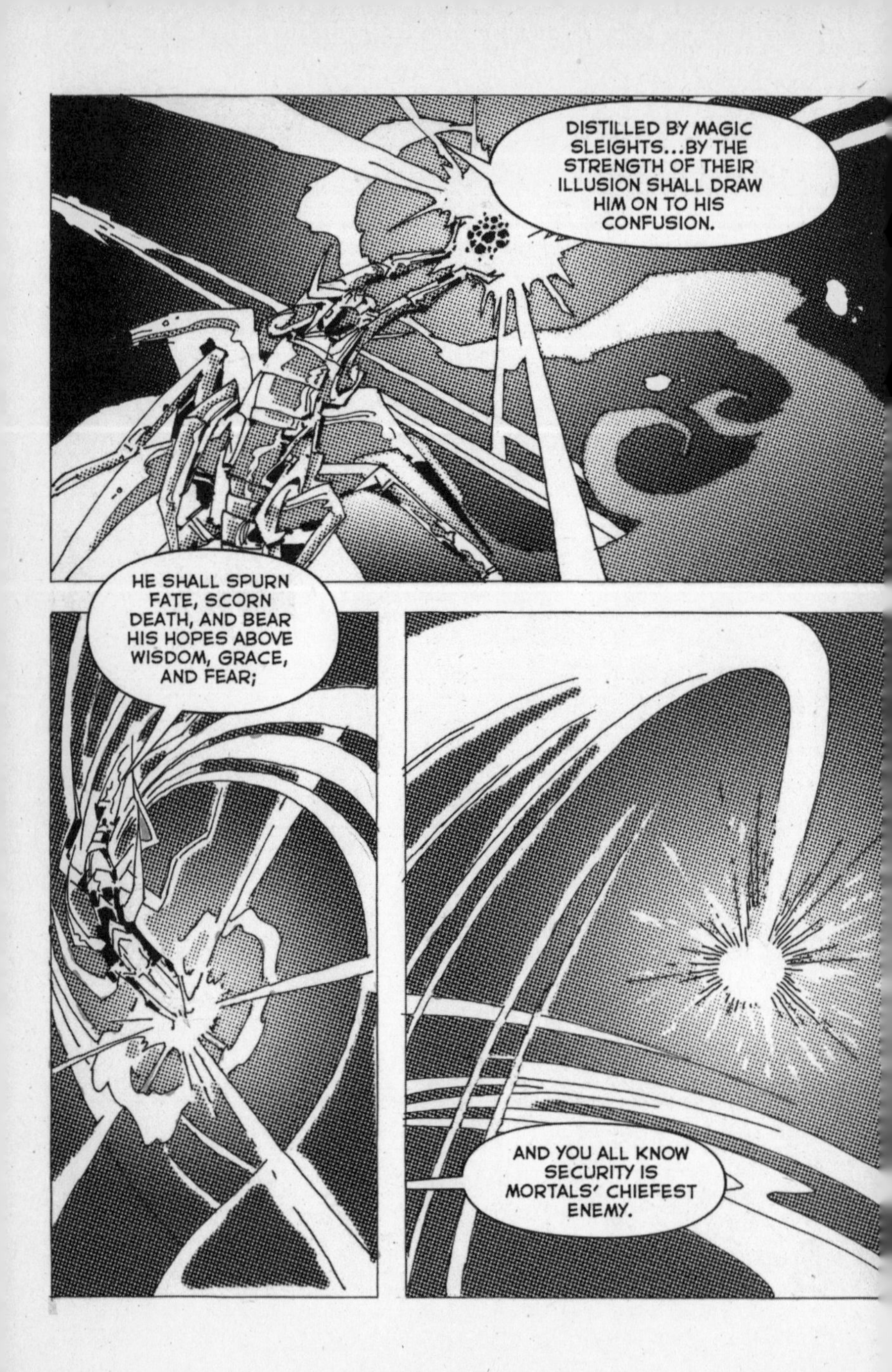
DISTILLED BY MAGIC SLEIGHTS...BY THE STRENGTH OF THEIR ILLUSION SHALL DRAW HIM ON TO HIS CONFUSION.
HE SHALL SPURN FATE, SCORN DEATH, AND BEAR HIS HOPES ABOVE WISDOM, GRACE, AND FEAR;
AND YOU ALL KNOW SECURITY IS MORTALS' CHIEFEST ENEMY.

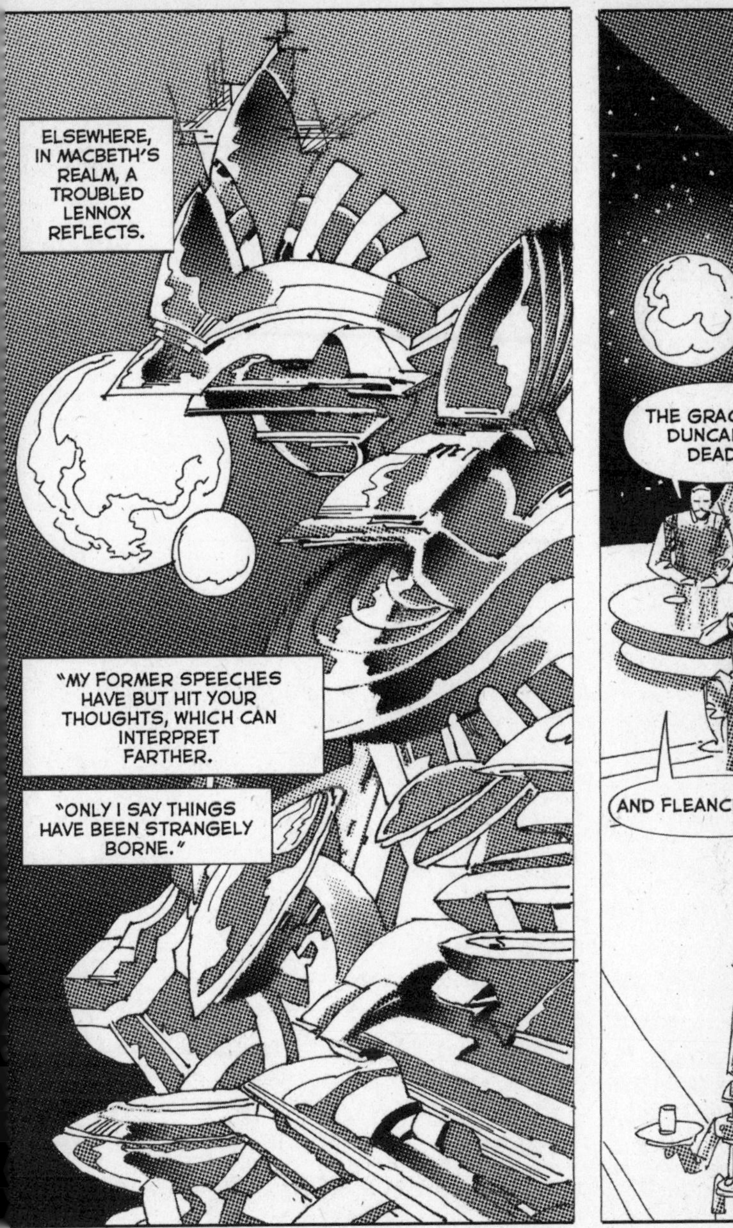
ELSEWHERE, IN MACBETH'S REALM, A TROUBLED LENNOX REFLECTS.
"MY FORMER SPEECHES HAVE BUT HIT YOUR THOUGHTS, WHICH CAN INTERPRET FARTHER.
"ONLY I SAY THINGS HAVE BEEN STRANGELY BORNE."

THE GRACIOUS DUNCAN... DEAD.
AND FLEANCE...FLED.

WHO CANNOT WANT THE THOUGHT HOW MONSTROUS IT WAS FOR MALCOLM AND FOR DONALBAIN...
...TO KILL THEIR GRACIOUS FATHER?
HOW IT DID GRIEVE MACBETH! DID HE NOT STRAIGHT, IN PIOUS RAGE, THE TWO DELINQUENTS TEAR?
WAS NOT THAT NOBLY DONE? AY, AND WISELY TOO.
HE HAS BORNE ALL THINGS WELL.
HAD HE DUNCAN'S SONS UNDER HIS KEY...
...THEY SHOULD FIND WHAT 'TWERE TO KILL A FATHER.

I HEAR MACDUFF LIVES IN DISGRACE.
SIR, CAN YOU TELL WHERE HE BESTOWS HIMSELF?
THE SON OF DUNCAN...
"...LIVES IN THE ENGLISH COURT, AND IS RECEIVED OF THE MOST PIOUS EDWARD...
"THITHER MACDUFF... TO PRAY THE HOLY KING UPON HIS AID.
"...TO WAKE NORTHUMBER-LAND AND WARLIKE SIWARD."

THAT BY THE HELP OF THESE WE MAY AGAIN...
...SLEEP FREE FROM BLOODY KNIVES.
THE KING... PREPARES FOR SOME ATTEMPT OF WAR.
SENT HE TO MACDUFF?
HE DID, AND WITH AN ABSOLUTE, "SIR, NOT I"...

YOU'LL RUE THE TIME THAT CLOGS ME WITH THIS ANSWER.
FLY TO THE COURT OF ENGLAND AND UNFOLD HIS MESSAGE ERE HE COME...
THAT A SWIFT BLESSING MAY SOON RETURN TO THIS OUR SUFFERING COUNTRY UNDER A HAND ACCURSED.
I'LL SEND MY PRAYERS WITH HIM.

"DOUBLE; DOUBLE TOIL AND TROUBLE, FIRE BURN AND CAULDRON BUBBLE...

THRICE THE BRINDLED CAT HATH MEWED.
THRICE, AND ONCE THE HEDGEPIG WHINED.
HARPIER CRIES: 'TIS TIME, 'TIS TIME!
ROUND ABOUT THE CAULDRON GO; IN THE POISONED ENTRAILS THROW,
TOAD, THAT UNDER COLD STONE DAYS AND NIGHT HAS THIRTY-ONE
SWELTERED VENOM SLEEPING GOT, BOIL THOU FIRST IN THE CHARMED POT.
"EYE OF NEWT, AND TOE OF FROG...
"...WOOL OF BAT, TONGUE OF DOG."

DOUBLE, DOUBLE TOIL AND TROUBLE, FIRE BURN AND CAULDRON BUBBLE.
EYE OF NEWT, AND TOE OF FROG, WOOL OF BAT, AND TONGUE OF DOG.
"LIKE A CHARM OF POWERFUL TROUBLE LIKE A HELLBROTH BOIL AND BUBBLE."
DOUBLE, DOUBLE TOIL AND TROUBLE, FIRE BURN AND CALDRON BUBBLE.

"SCALE OF A DRAGON, TOOTH OF WOLF, WITCH'S MUMMY, MAW AND GULF...
"OF THE RAVINED SALT-SEA SHARK, ROOT OF HEMLOCK DIGGED I' TH' DARK..."
SLIVERED IN THE MOON'S ECLIPSE, NOSE OF TURK, AND TARTAR'S LIPS...
"FINGER OF A BIRTH-STRANGLED BABE DITCH-DELIVERED BY A DRAB..."

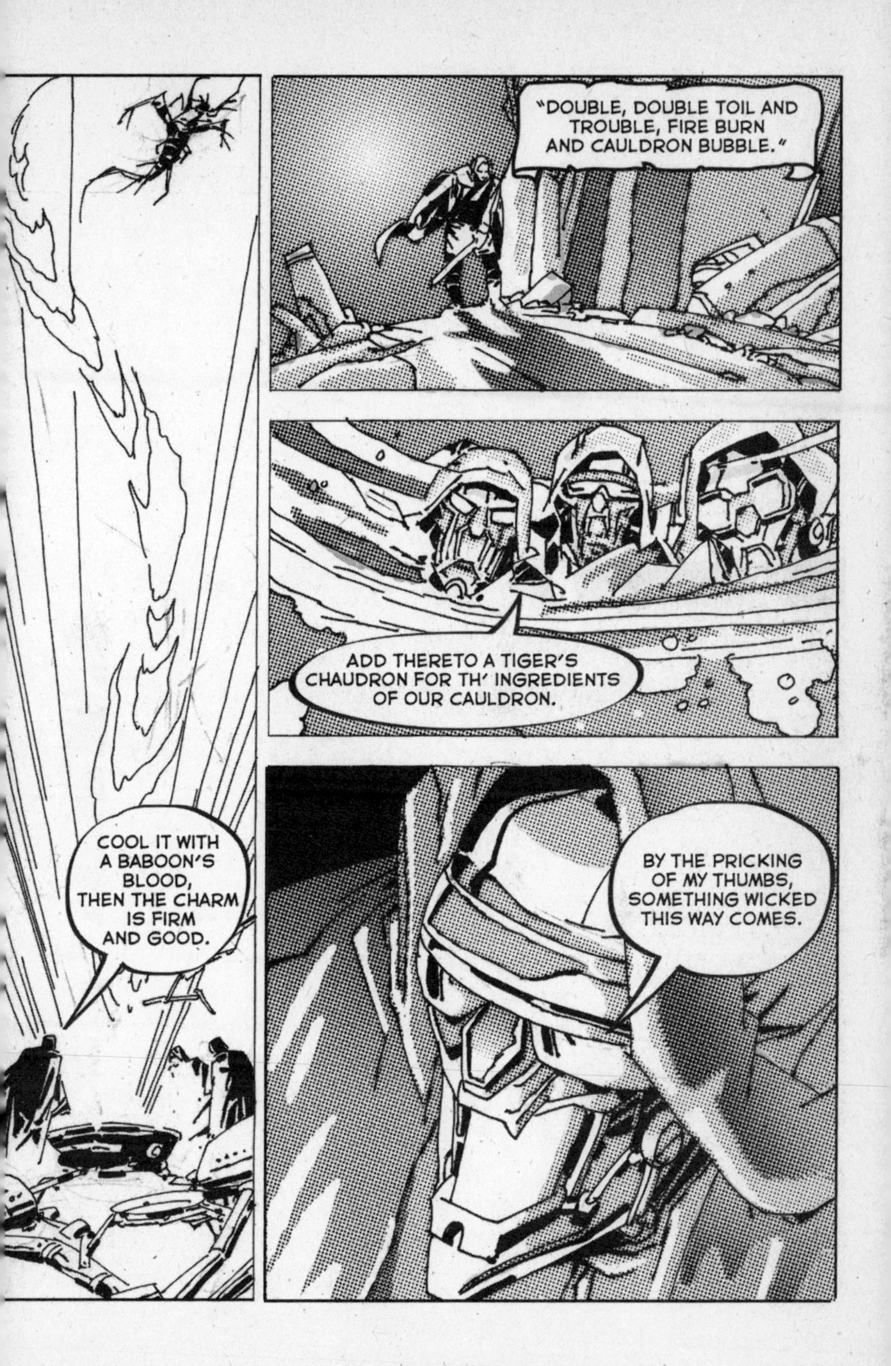
"DOUBLE, DOUBLE TOIL AND TROUBLE, FIRE BURN AND CAULDRON BUBBLE."
ADD THERETO A TIGER'S CHAUDRON FOR TH' INGREDIENTS OF OUR CAULDRON.
COOL IT WITH A BABOON'S BLOOD, THEN THE CHARM IS FIRM AND GOOD.
BY THE PRICKING OF MY THUMBS, SOMETHING WICKED THIS WAY COMES.

OPEN LOCKS, WHOEVER KNOCKS!
NOK NOK
HOW NOW, YOU MIDNIGHT HAGS, WHAT IS IT YOU DO?
A DEED WITHOUT A NAME, MACBETH.
EVEN TILL DESTRUCTION SICKEN, ANSWER ME TO WHAT I ASK YOU.

SPEAK.
DEMAND.
WE'LL ANSWER.
SAY IF THOU'DST RATHER HEAR IT FROM OUR MOUTHS OR FROM OUR MASTERS.
CALL 'EM. LET ME SEE 'EM.
POUR IN SOW'S BLOOD, THAT HATH EATEN HER NINE FARROW; GREASE THAT'S SWEATEN.
COME, HIGH OR LOW THYSELF AND OFFICE DEFTLY SHOW.

MACBETH, BEWARE MACDUFF, THANE OF FIFE.
DISMISS ME. ENOUGH.
FOR THY GOOD CAUTION THANKS.
BUT ONE WORD MORE...
HE WILL NOT BE COMMANDED.
HERE'S ANOTHER MORE POTENT THAN THE FIRST.
BE BLOODY, BOLD, AND RESOLUTE.

LAUGH TO SCORN THE POW'R OF MAN, FOR NONE OF WOMAN BORN SHALL HARM MACBETH.
MACDUFF, WHAT NEED I FEAR OF THEE? BUT YET I'LL MAKE ASSURANCE DOUBLE SURE... THOU SHALL NOT LIVE.
WHAT IS THIS?

MACBETH SHALL NEVER VANQUISHED BE...
...UNTIL GREAT BIRNAM WOOD TO HIGH DUNSINANE HILL SHALL COME AGAINST HIM.
THAT WILL NEVER BE. WHO CAN IMPRESS THE FOREST, BID THE TREE UNFIX HIS EARTHBOUND ROOT?
OF BIRNAM RISE, AND OUR HIGH-PLACED MACBETH...SHALL LIVE THE LEASE OF NATURE.
WHERE ARE THEY?

GONE?
COME IN, WITHOUT THERE!
LENNOX, I DID HEAR THE GALLOPING OF A HORSE. WHO WAS'T CAME BY?
MACDUFF IS FLED TO ENGLAND.
FLED TO ENGLAND?
AYE, MY GOOD LORD.

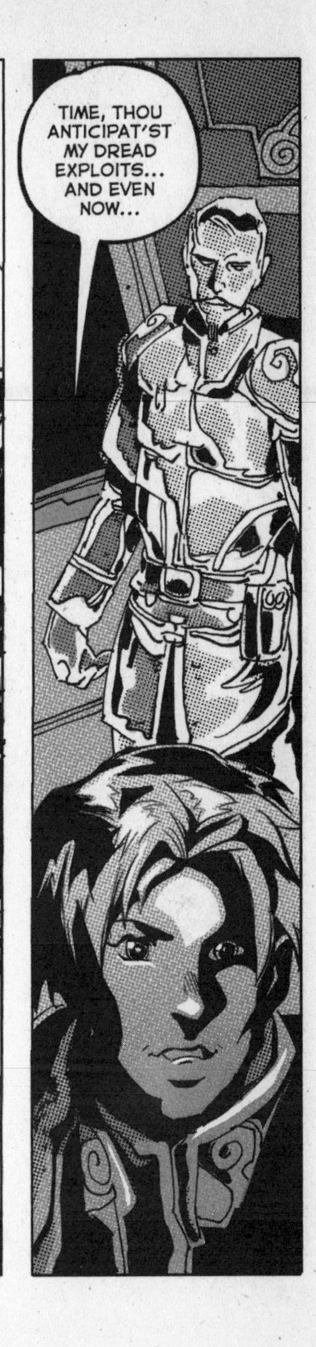
TIME, THOU ANTICIPAT'ST MY DREAD EXPLOITS... AND EVEN NOW...

THE CASTLE OF MACDUFF I WILL SURPRISE...GIVE TO TH'EDGE O'TH' SWORD HIS WIFE, HIS BABES!
NO BOASTING LIKE A FOOL; THIS DEED I'LL DO BEFORE THIS PURPOSE COOL.
WHERE ARE THESE GENTLEMEN? COME, LENNOX, BRING ME WHERE THEY ARE.
MEANWHILE AT CASTLE MACDUFF...
WHAT HAD HE DONE TO MAKE HIM FLY THE LAND?

YOU MUST HAVE PATIENCE, LADY MACDUFF.
HE HAD NONE, HIS FLIGHT WAS MADNESS.
YOU KNOW NOT WHETHER IT WAS HIS WISDOM OR HIS FEAR.
WISDOM, ROSS? TO LEAVE HIS WIFE, TO LEAVE HIS BABES, FROM WHENCE HIMSELF DOES FLY?
HE LOVES US NOT.

ALL IS THE FEAR AND NOTHING IS THE LOVE...
MY DEAREST COZ, I PRAY YOU SCHOOL YOURSELF.
BUT CRUEL ARE THE TIMES...WHEN WE HOLD RUMOR FROM WHAT WE FEAR, YET KNOW NOT WHAT WE FEAR...
EACH WAY AND NONE. I TAKE MY LEAVE OF YOU ...BUT I'LL BE HERE AGAIN.

MY PRETTY COUSIN, BLESSING UPON YOU.
FATHERED HE IS, AND YET HE'S FATHERLESS.
I TAKE MY LEAVE AT ONCE.
HOW WILT THOU DO FOR A FATHER?
NAY, HOW WILT THOU DO FOR A HUSBAND?
WHY, I CAN BUY ME TWENTY AT ANY MARKET.
THEN YOU'LL BUY 'EM TO SELL AGAIN.

NOW GOD HELP THEE, POOR MONKEY! BUT HOW WILT THOU DO FOR A FATHER?
IF HE WERE DEAD, YOU'D WEEP FOR HIM.
IF YOU WOULD NOT, IT WERE A GOOD SIGN...
...THAT I SHOULD QUICKLY HAVE A NEW FATHER.
SSKKKK
WHAT ARE THESE FACES?
WHERE IS YOUR HUSBAND?

I HOPE IN NO PLACE SO UNSANCTIFIED WHERE SUCH AS THOU MAYST FIND HIM.
HE'S A TRAITOR.
THOU LIEST, THOU SHAG-EAR'D VILLAIN.
WHAT, YOU EGG!
YOUNG FRY OF TREACHERY!

HE HAS KILLED ME, MOTHER.
RUN AWAY, I PRAY YOU!

"LET US SEEK OUT SOME DESOLATE SHADE, MACDUFF..."
IN ENGLAND...
AND THERE WEEP OUR SAD BOSOMS EMPTY.
LET US RATHER HOLD FAST THE MORAL SWORD, MALCOLM...

NEW SORROWS STRIKE HEAVEN ON THE FACE.
MACDUFF, THIS TYRANT, WHOSE SOLE NAME TONGUES, WAS ONCE THOUGHT HONEST...
YOU HAVE LOVED HIM WELL; HE HATH NOT TOUCHED YOU YET.
YOU MAY DESERVE OF HIM THROUGH ME...TO APPEASE AN ANGRY GOD.

I AM NOT TREACHEROUS.
BUT MACBETH IS.

I HAVE LOST MY HOPES.
...
WHY LEFT YOU WIFE AND CHILD, WITHOUT LEAVE-TAKING?
LET NOT MY JEALOUSIES BE YOUR DISHONORS...
...BUT MINE OWN SAFETIES.

BLEED, BLEED, POOR COUNTRY!
FARE THEE WELL, LORD. I WOULD NOT BE THE VILLAIN THAT THOU THINK'ST.
BE NOT OFFENDED, OUR COUNTRY WEEPS, IT BLEEDS...
...AND EACH NEW DAY A GASH IS ADDED TO HER WOUNDS.
HERE FROM GRACIOUS ENGLAND HAVE I OFFER OF GOODLY THOUSANDS.
MORE SUFFER...

A DEVIL IN EVILS IS MACBETH.
I GRANT HIM...
SMACKING OF EVERY SIN THAT HAS A NAME.
BOUNDLESS INTEMPERANCE IN NATURE IS A TYRANNY.
IT HATH BEEN THE UNTIMELY EMPTYING OF THE HAPPY THRONE AND THE FALL OF MANY KINGS.

AND, MACDUFF, MY MORE-HAVING WOULD BE AS A SAUCE TO MAKE ME HUNGER MORE...
O SCOTLAND, SCOTLAND!
IF SUCH A ONE BE FIT TO GOVERN, SPEAK. I AM AS I HAVE SPOKEN.
THESE EVILS THOU REPEAT'ST UPON THYSELF HATH BANISHED ME FROM SCOTLAND.

MACDUFF, CHILD OF INTEGRITY...
WHAT I AM TRULY IS THINE AND MY POOR COUNTRY'S TO COMMAND.
NOW WE'LL TOGETHER.
SEE WHO COMES HERE.

MY EVER GENTLE COUSIN, ROSS, WELCOME HITHER.
SIR, AMEN.
STANDS SCOTLAND WHERE IT DID?
ALAS, POOR COUNTRY, IT CANNOT BE CALLED OUR MOTHER BUT OUR GRAVE.
O, RELATION TOO NICE, AND YET TOO TRUE!
WHAT'S THE NEWEST GRIEF?
THAT OF AN HOUR'S AGE DOTH HISS THE SPEAKER; EACH MINUTE TEEMS A NEW ONE.

ROSS, HOW DOES MY WIFE? AND ALL MY CHILDREN?
YOUR CASTLE IS SURPRISED, YOUR WIFE AND BABES SAVAGELY SLAUGHTERED.
MACDUFF, LET NOT YOUR EARS DESPISE MY TONGUE FOREVER.
MERCIFUL HEAVEN.

BE COMFORTED.
LET'S MAKE US MEDICINES OF OUR GREAT REVENGE. TO CURE THIS DEADLY GRIEF.
I SHALL DO SO.
HEAVEN REST THEM NOW.

BRING THIS FIEND OF SCOTLAND WITHIN MY SWORD'S LENGTH.
OUR POWER IS READY. THE NIGHT IS LONG THAT NEVER FINDS THE DAY.
IN MACBETH'S CASTLE...

YOU SEE HER EYES ARE OPEN.
AY, BUT THEIR SENSE ARE SHUT.
WHAT IS IT SHE DOES NOW? LOOK...

...HOW SHE RUBS HER HANDS.
IT IS AN ACCUSTOMED ACTION WITH HER...
I HAVE KNOWN HER TO CONTINUE IN THIS A QUARTER OF AN HOUR.
YET HERE'S A SPOT.
OUT DAMNED SPOT! OUT, I SAY!
YET WHO WOULD HAVE THOUGHT THE OLD MAN TO HAVE HAD SO MUCH BLOOD IN HIM?

THE THANE OF FIFE HAD A WIFE. WHERE IS SHE NOW?
HERE'S THE SMELL OF THE BLOOD STILL. OH, OH, OH!
WASH YOUR HANDS ...BANQUO'S BURIED.
HE CANNOT COME OUT OF HIS GRAVE.
TO BED, TO BED...
COME, COME, COME, COME, GIVE ME YOUR HAND.

WHAT'S DONE CANNOT BE UNDONE. TO BED, TO BED, TO BED.
UNNATURAL DEEDS DO BREED UNNATURAL TROUBLES... GOD, GOD FORGIVE US ALL.
A FEW DAYS LATER, NEAR MACBETH'S CASTLE DUNSINANE...
THE ENGLISH POWER IS NEAR, LED ON BY MALCOLM, HIS UNCLE SIWARD, AND THE GOOD MACDUFF.
REVENGES BURN IN THEM...

NEAR BIRNAM WOOD SHALL WE MEET THEM...
...THAT WAY THEY ARE COMING.
WHAT DOES THE TYRANT?
GREAT DUNSINANE HE STRONGLY FORTIFIES.
SOME SAY HE'S MAD; OTHERS CALL IT VALIANT FURY.

INSIDE THE CASTLE KEEP...
BRING ME NO MORE REPORTS. LET THEM FLY ALL.
THE SPIRITS THAT KNOW...HAVE PRONOUNCED ME THUS:
"NO MAN THAT'S BORN OF WOMAN SHALL E'ER HAVE POWER UPON THEE."
THOU CREAM-FACED LOON! WHERE GOT'ST THOU WITH THAT GOOSE LOOK?
THERE IS TEN THOUSAND...
GEESE, VILLAIN?
SOLDIERS, SIR.
TAKE THY FACE HENCE.

AS HONOR, LOVE, OBEDIENCE, TROOPS OF FRIENDS, I MUST NOT LOOK TO HAVE.
BUT, IN THEIR STEAD, CURSES NOT LOUD BUT DEEP.
HOW DOES YOUR PATIENT, DOCTOR?
SHE IS TROUBLED WITH THICK-COMING FANCIES THAT KEEP HER FROM HER REST.
CANST THOU NOT MINISTER TO A MIND DISEASED...

AND CLEANSE THAT WHICH WEIGHS UPON THE HEART?
THEREIN THE PATIENT MUST MINISTER TO HIMSELF.
THROW PHYSIC TO THE DOGS, I'LL NONE OF IT.
AY, MY GOOD LORD. YOUR ROYAL PREPARA-TION MAKES US HEAR SOME-THING.
I WILL NOT BE AFRAID OF DEATH AND BANE TILL BIRNAM FOREST COME TO DUNSINANE.

"OUR CASTLE'S STRENGTH WILL LAUGH A SIEGE TO SCORN."
EEEEEEEEE
WHAT IS THAT NOISE?
IT IS THE CRY OF WOMEN, MY GOOD LORD.
I HAVE ALMOST FORGOT THE TASTE OF FEARS.
"DIRENESS, FAMILIAR TO MY SLAUGHTEROUS THOUGHTS, CANNOT ONCE START ME."

THE QUEEN, MY LORD, IS DEAD.
SHE...
TOMORROW, AND TOMORROW, AND TOMORROW CREEPS INTO HIS PETTY PACE FROM DAY TO DAY...
...TO THE LAST SYLLABLE OF RE-CORDED TIME...
...AND ALL OUR YESTERDAYS HAVE LIGHTED FOOLS THE WAY TO DUSTY DEATH.
OUT, OUT, BRIEF CANDLE, LIFE'S BUT A WALKING SHADOW, A POOR PLAYER
...THAT FRETS HIS HOUR UPON THE STAGE AND THEN IS HEARD NO MORE.
IT IS A TALE TOLD BY AN IDIOT, FULL OF SOUND AND FURY, SIGNIFYING NOTHING.
MY LORD, AS I DID STAND MY WATCH UPON THE HILL...

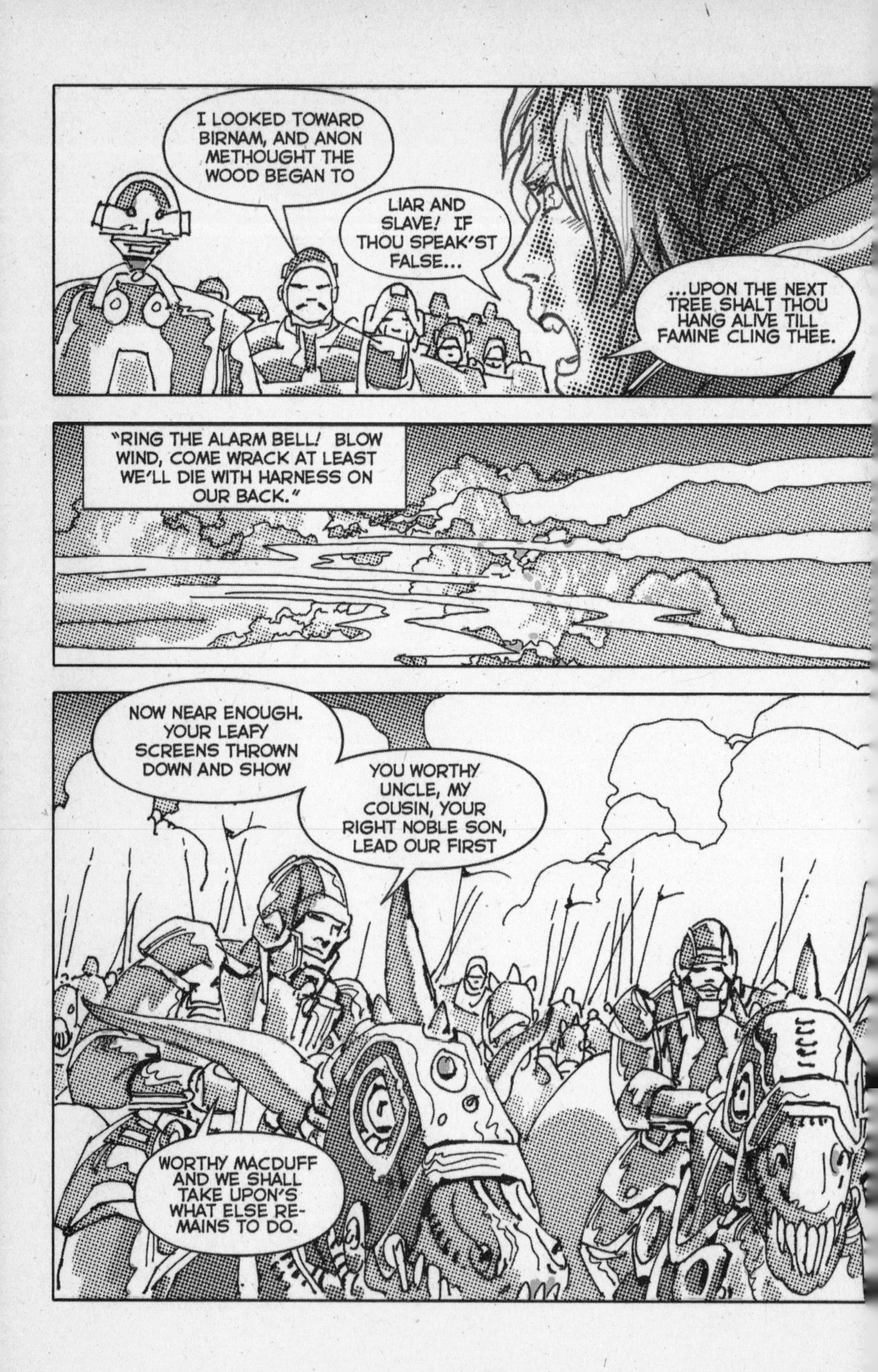
I LOOKED TOWARD BIRNAM, AND ANON METHOUGHT THE WOOD BEGAN TO
LIAR AND SLAVE! IF THOU SPEAK'ST FALSE...
...UPON THE NEXT TREE SHALT THOU HANG ALIVE TILL FAMINE CLING THEE.
"RING THE ALARM BELL! BLOW WIND, COME WRACK AT LEAST WE'LL DIE WITH HARNESS ON OUR BACK."
NOW NEAR ENOUGH. YOUR LEAFY SCREENS THROWN DOWN AND SHOW
YOU WORTHY UNCLE, MY COUSIN, YOUR RIGHT NOBLE SON, LEAD OUR FIRST
WORTHY MACDUFF AND WE SHALL TAKE UPON'S WHAT ELSE RE-MAINS TO DO.

"THEY HAVE TIED ME TO A STAKE. I CANNOT FLY...
"WHAT'S HE THAT WAS NOT BORN OF WOMAN? SUCH A ONE AM I TO FEAR, OR NONE."
WHAT IS THY NAME?
MY NAME'S MACBETH.
"THE DEVIL HIMSELF COULD NOT PRONOUNCE A TITLE MORE HATEFUL TO MINE EAR."
NO, NOR MORE FEARFUL.

WHY SHOULD I PLAY THE ROMAN FOOL AND DIE ON MINE OWN SWORD?
TURN, HELL-HOUND, TURN!
OF ALL MEN ELSE I HAVE AVOIDED THEE, MACDUFF. BUT GET THEE BACK.
MY SOUL IS TOO MUCH CHARGED WITH BLOOD OF THINE ALREADY.
I HAVE NO WORDS; MY VOICE IS IN MY SWORD.
I BEAR A CHARMED LIFE, WHICH MUST NOT YIELD TO ONE OF WOMAN BORN.

DESPAIR THY CHARM, AND LET THE ANGEL WHOM THOU STILL HAST SERVED TELL THEE.
MACDUFF WAS FROM HIS MOTHER'S WOMB UNTIMELY RIPPED.
ACCURSED BE THE TONGUE THAT TELLS ME SO... I'LL NOT FIGHT WITH THEE.
THEN YIELD THEE COWARD...
...AND LIVE TO BE THE SHOW.
LAY ON, MACDUFF...
...AND DAMNED BE HIM THAT FIRST CRIES...
"HOLD, ENOUGH!" AKK!

HAIL, KING MALCOLM, FOR SO THOU ART. BEHOLD THE USURPER'S CURSED HEAD. HAIL, KING OF SCOTLAND.
HAIL, KING OF SCOTLAND!
MY THANES AND KINSMEN, HENCEFORTH BE EARLS, THE FIRST THAT EVER SCOTLAND NAMED.
THANKS TO ALL. AND TO EACH...WE INVITE TO SEE US CROWNED AT SCONE.

The making of
WILLIAM SHAKESPEARE'S
MACBETH

"One advantage this book has is its length.
I had the time and space to present a fuller version of *Macbeth*."
—Arthur Byron Cover

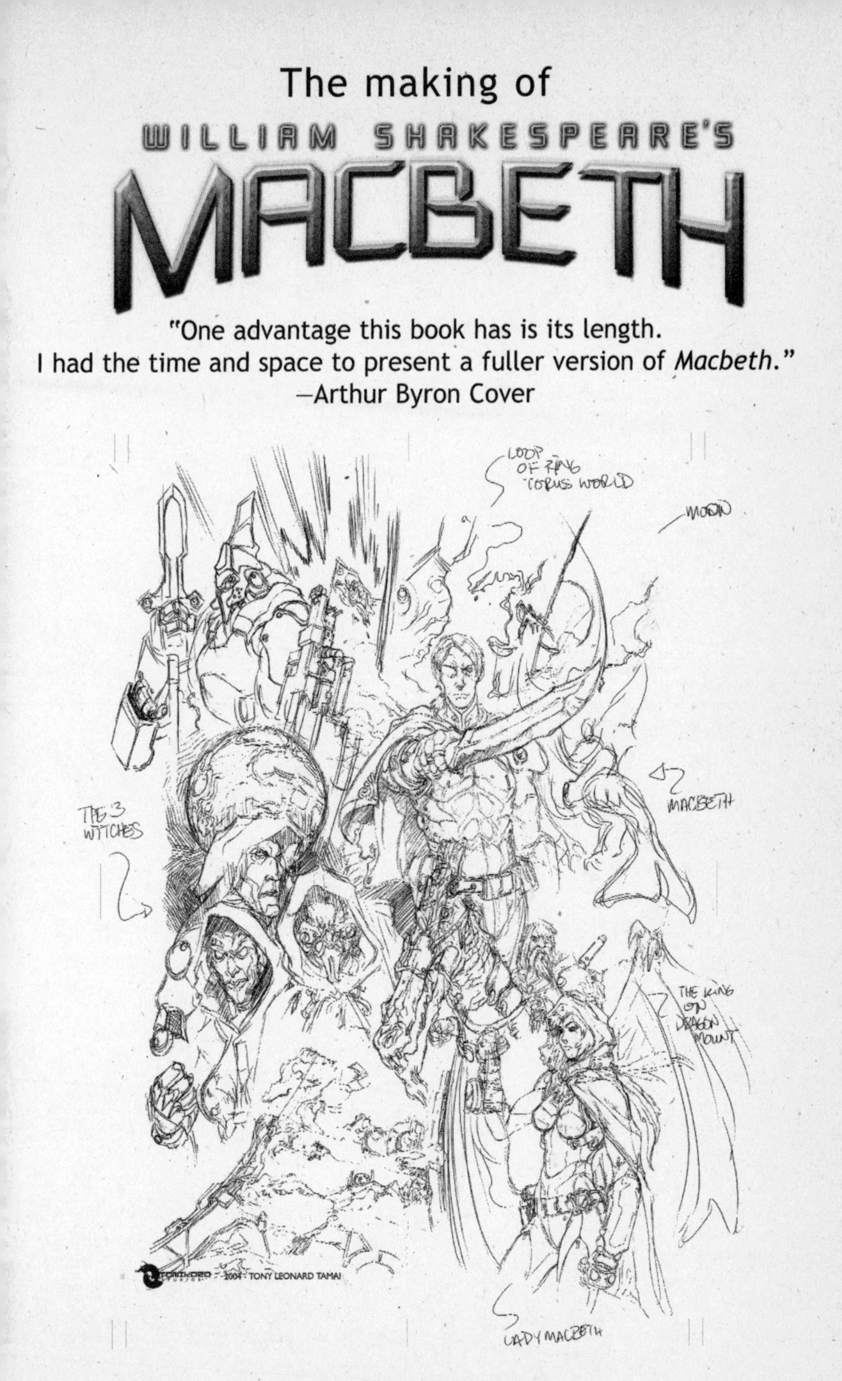

An early cover design with notes

Arthur Byron Cover talks about his adaptation of

As both a writer and a reader, I tend to view fiction in terms of storyboards, as if the tale I read is a cross between a comic and a movie. I mentally fill in the gaps between the panels.

To a great extent adapting *Macbeth* into the graphic novel medium was a creative exercise in visualization. I did research of course, and got ideas from descriptions on the Internet. As for the science-fiction elements, I simply attempted to imagine a production of the play as if it occurred on a world that is a combination of the settings of Larry Niven's *Ringworld* and Anne McCaffery's *Pern* novels. I tried to imagine the actors speaking in a non-declamatory style, so that they would have the opportunity to perform the little bits of business that would theoretically illuminate their character.

The most important resource I consulted, however, more important than my own imagination I fear, was *Asimov's Guide to Shakespeare*.

The great virtue of Isaac Asimov's scholarship is his hard-headed practical approach. He tells you the science and history of the times, both as it was believed to be and as it actually was.

I consulted his essay on *Macbeth* every time I reached a new scene and found it constantly illuminating. If the reader finds himself interested in reading more Shakespeare after he has finished reading this version of *Macbeth*, he could do worse, far worse, than find a copy of *Asimov's Guide to Shakespeare*.

Arthur used as his source the Pelican Shakespeare edition of *Macbeth*.

THE EARLY STAGES OF *MACBETH*

Comics have a long history of having groups of artists collaborate, either formally in a studio, or from separate locations. Tony Leonard Tamai was assisted on *Macbeth* by respected comics artist Alex Niño, who helped on the second half of the adaptation. Tony created pencil breakdowns and Alex worked off Tony's layouts to create finished art. In this collaboration, we see how another artist interpreted the scenes.

Here is a rare behind-the-scenes look at Tony Leonard Tamai's pencil breakdowns of the opening scene of *Macbeth*. In these sketches the full range of the artist's approach to the developing finished story page is evident. Note the sketches for sound effects, the crude drawings of people beside more finished renderings, and the roughly sketched panel borders. Some pages show some preliminary tone work, others do not. Compare these pages with the finished ones earlier in the book.

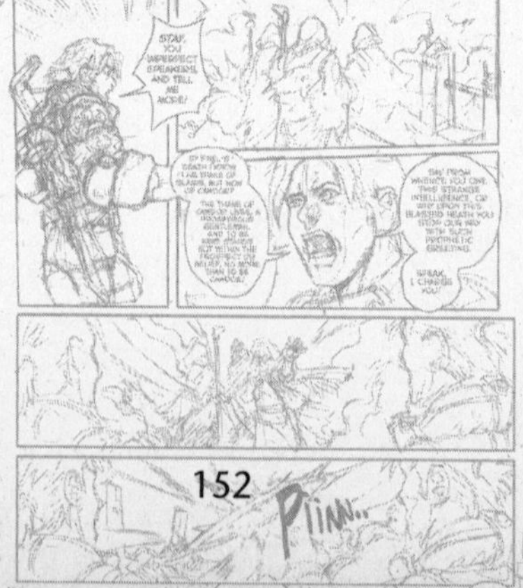

STARDATE: 1040. THE FORCES OF KING DUNCAN ARE ENGAGED IN BATTLE AGAINST THOSE OF THE REBEL MACDONWALD. LEADING THE CHARGE IS THE KING'S LOYAL SERVANT, THE THANE MACBETH..
BOOM!
"WHEN SHALL WE MEET AGAIN? -IN THUNDER, LIGHTNING, OR IN RAIN?"

BOOM!!
WHEN ALL THE HURLY-BURLY'S DONE, WHEN THE BATTLE'S LOST AND WON..
POM
TCHOOM
W3
W2
W1
THAT WILL BE ERE THE SET OF THE SUN.
WHERE THE PLACE?
UPON THE HEATH..

DOOM!
FAIR IS FOUL, AND FOUL IS FAIR. HOVER THROUGH THE FOG AND FILTHY AIR..
-ARRG!

WHAT BLOODY MAN IS THAT?
HAIL BRAVE FRIEND. SAY TO THE KING THE KNOWLEDGE OF THE BROIL AS THOU DIDST LEAVE IT.
THE MERCILESS MACDONWALD SHOWED LIKE A REBEL'S WHORE. BUT ALL'S TOO WEAK-
-CHIG!
FOR BRAVE MACBETH -WELL BE DESERVES THAT NAME- DISDAINING FORTUNE, WITH HIS BRANDISHED STEEL...

WHICH SMOKED WITH BLOODY EXECUTION LIKE VALOR'S MINION CARVED OUT HIS PASSAGE..
-TILL HE FACED THE SLAVE..
WHEW
WHICH NE'ER SHOOK HANDS NOR BADE FAREWELL TO HIM..

SHING
TILL HE UNSEAMED HIM FROM THE NAVE TO 'TH CHAPS AND FIXED HIS HEAD UPON OUR BATTLEMENTS.
PAGE - 6 ROUGH

O VALIENT COUSIN, WORTHY GENTLEMAN!
I AM FAINT. -MY GASHES CRY FOR HELP..
SO WELL THY WORDS BECOME THEE AS THY WOUNDS. THEY SMACK OF HONOR BOTH. -GO GET HIM SURGEONS.
WHO COMES HERE?
THE WORTHY THANE OF ROSS!
GOD SAVE THE KING!

TONY'S TOOLS

Tony does all his finished art digitally. Here and in the following eight pages, we see reproductions from his computer screen showing the different stages.

HOW TONY WORKS

Tony uses a combination of Painter 6, Photoshop CS, and comics software produced in Japan. Here, the "rough image" is worked out loosely in the data. He works in layers and can fully manipulate the image.

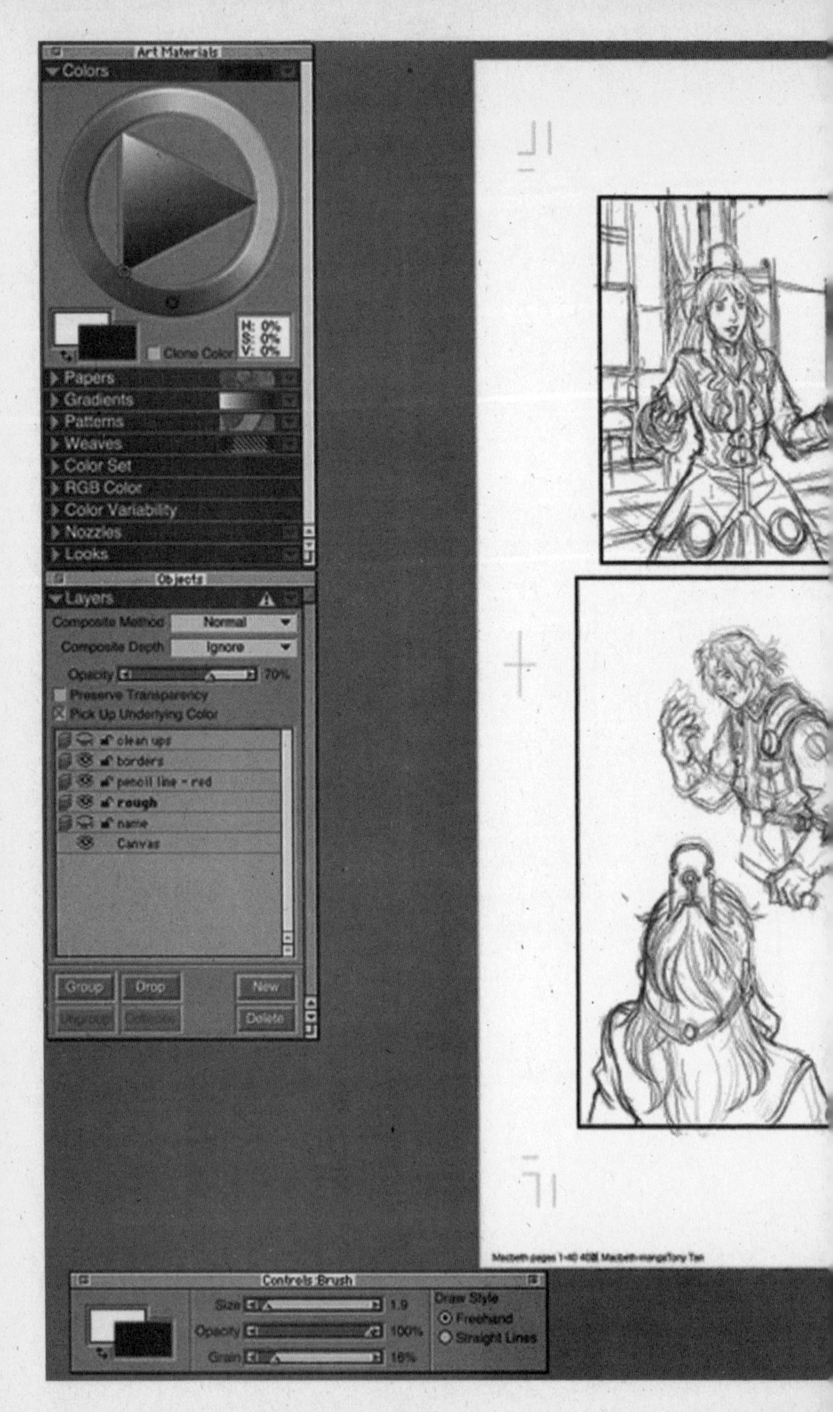

Art Materials
Colors
H: 0%
S: 0%
V: 0%
Clone Color
Papers
Gradients
Patterns
Weaves
Color Set
RGB Color
Color Variability
Nozzles
Looks
Objects
Layers
Composite Method
Normal
Composite Depth
Ignore
Opacity
70%
Preserve Transparency
Pick Up Underlying Color
clean ups
borders
pencil line - red
rough
name
Canvas
Group
Drop
New
Delete
Controls:Brush
Size
1.9
Opacity
100%
Grain
16%
Draw Style
Freehand
Straight Lines

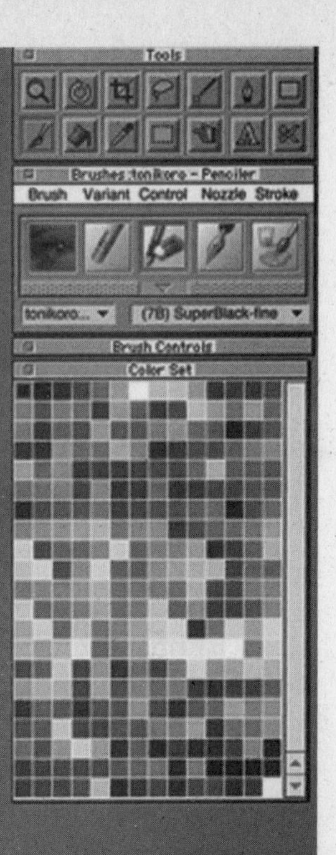

Once composition and placement are worked out, Tony refines the image on other layers, using the "rough" as a template.

Here Tony begins inking. Though he likes inking by hand, inking digitally is useful because it's easy to make corrections. There's no white out—only the tablet and the command CMND+Z.

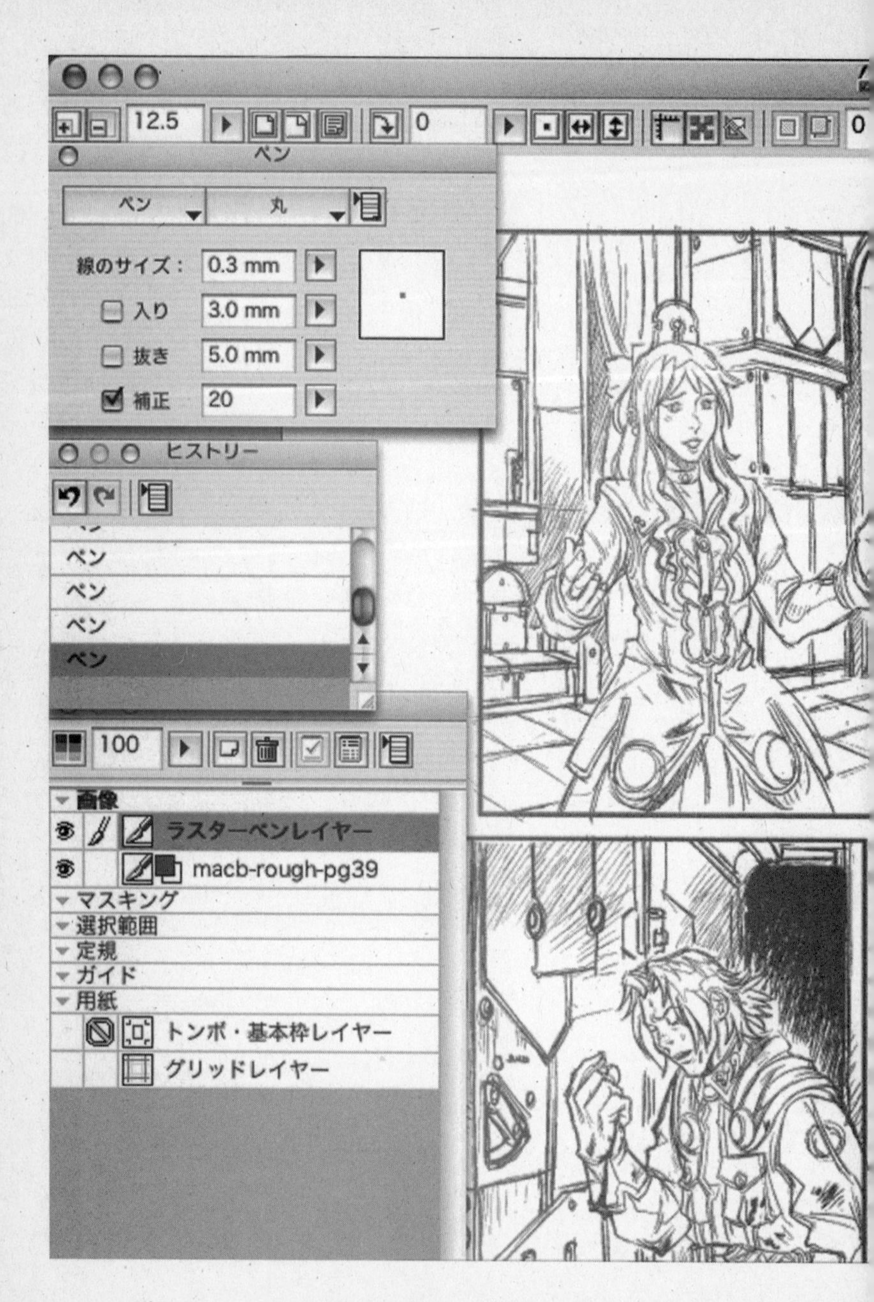

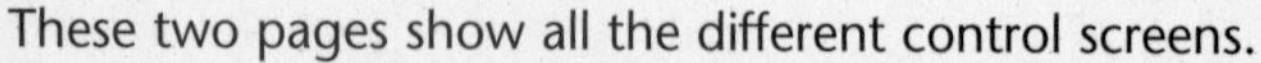

These two pages show all the different control screens.

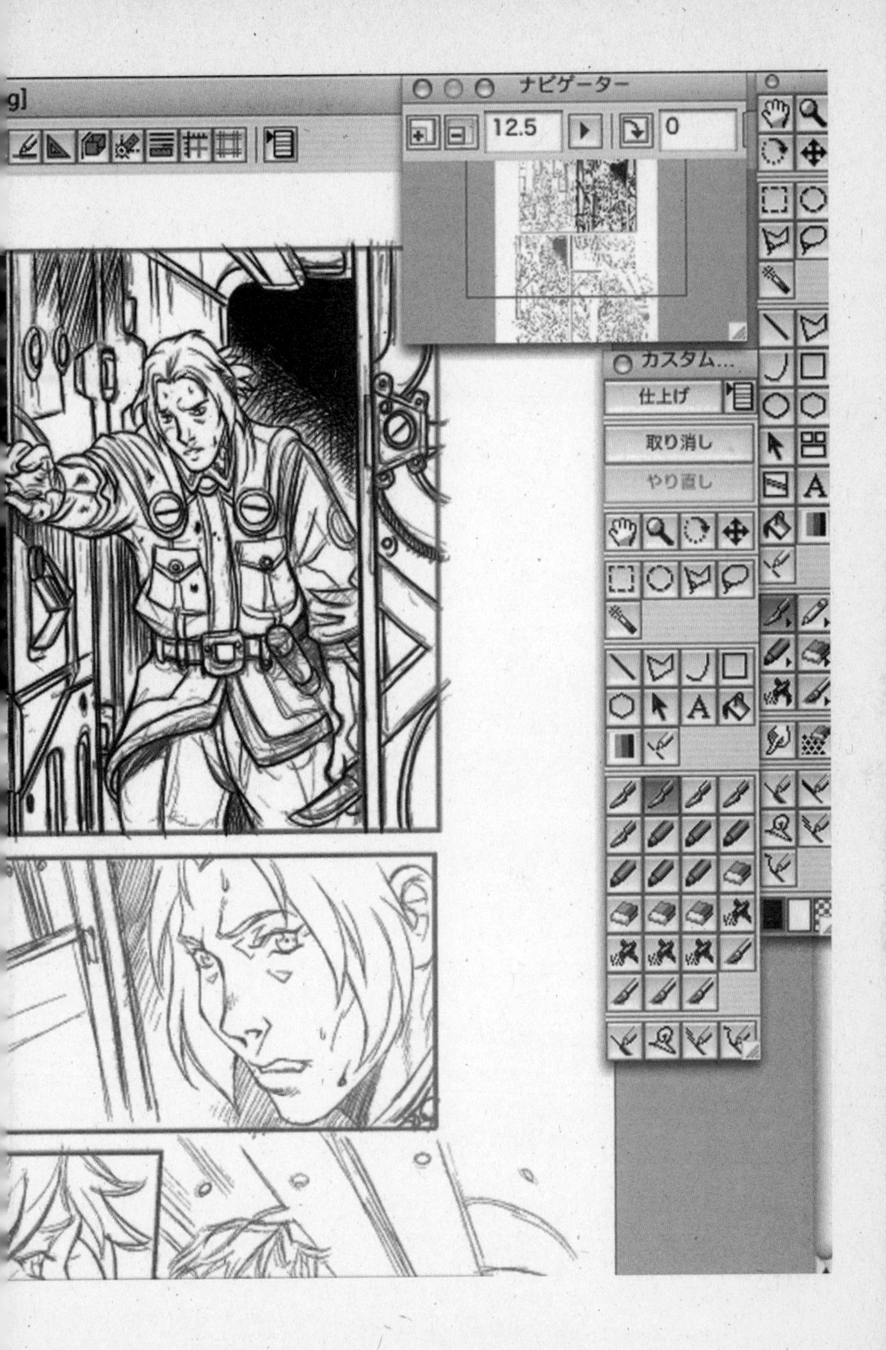
g]
ナビゲーター
12.5
0
カスタム...
仕上げ
取り消し
やり直し

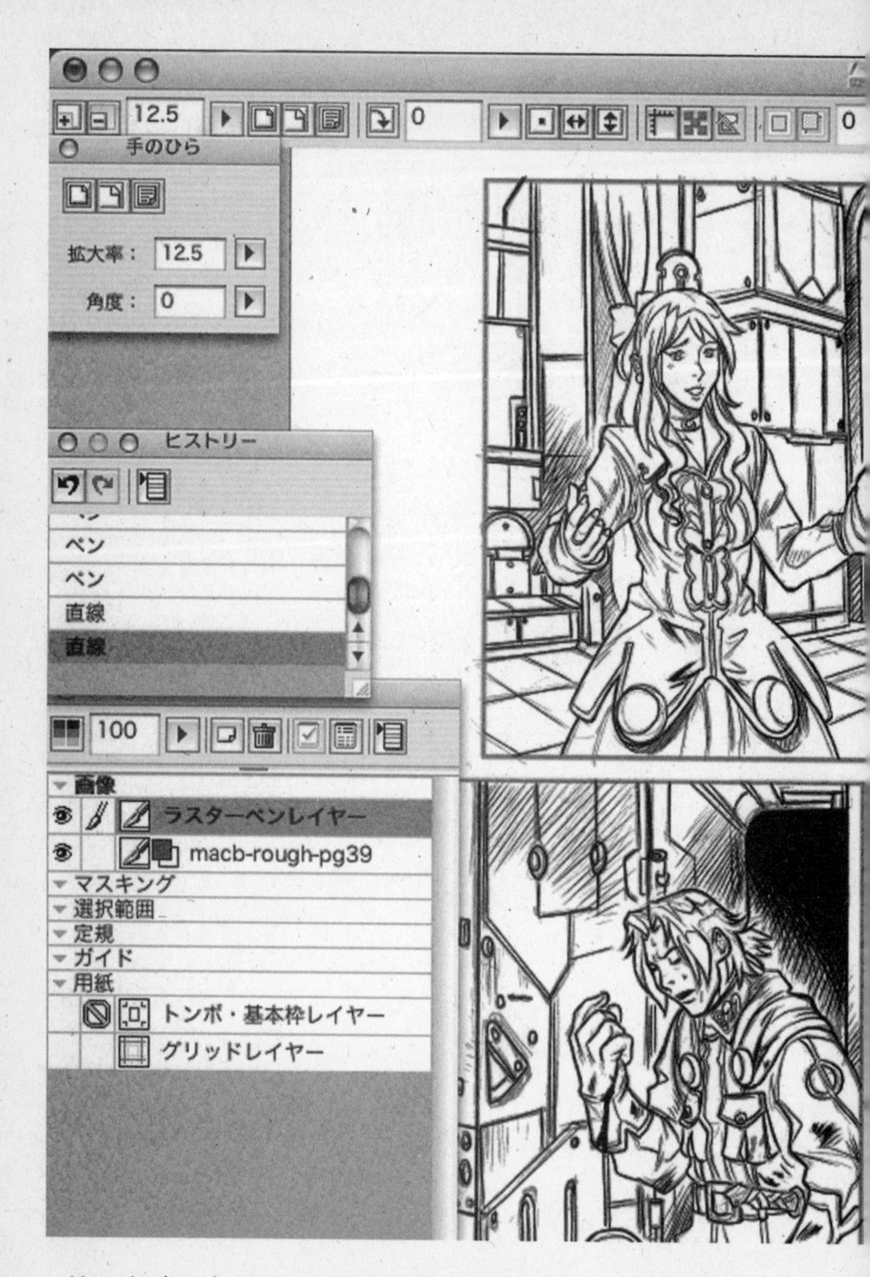

Here is the almost complete art. Tones will be placed in layers and the finished art with text will be sent to the editor.

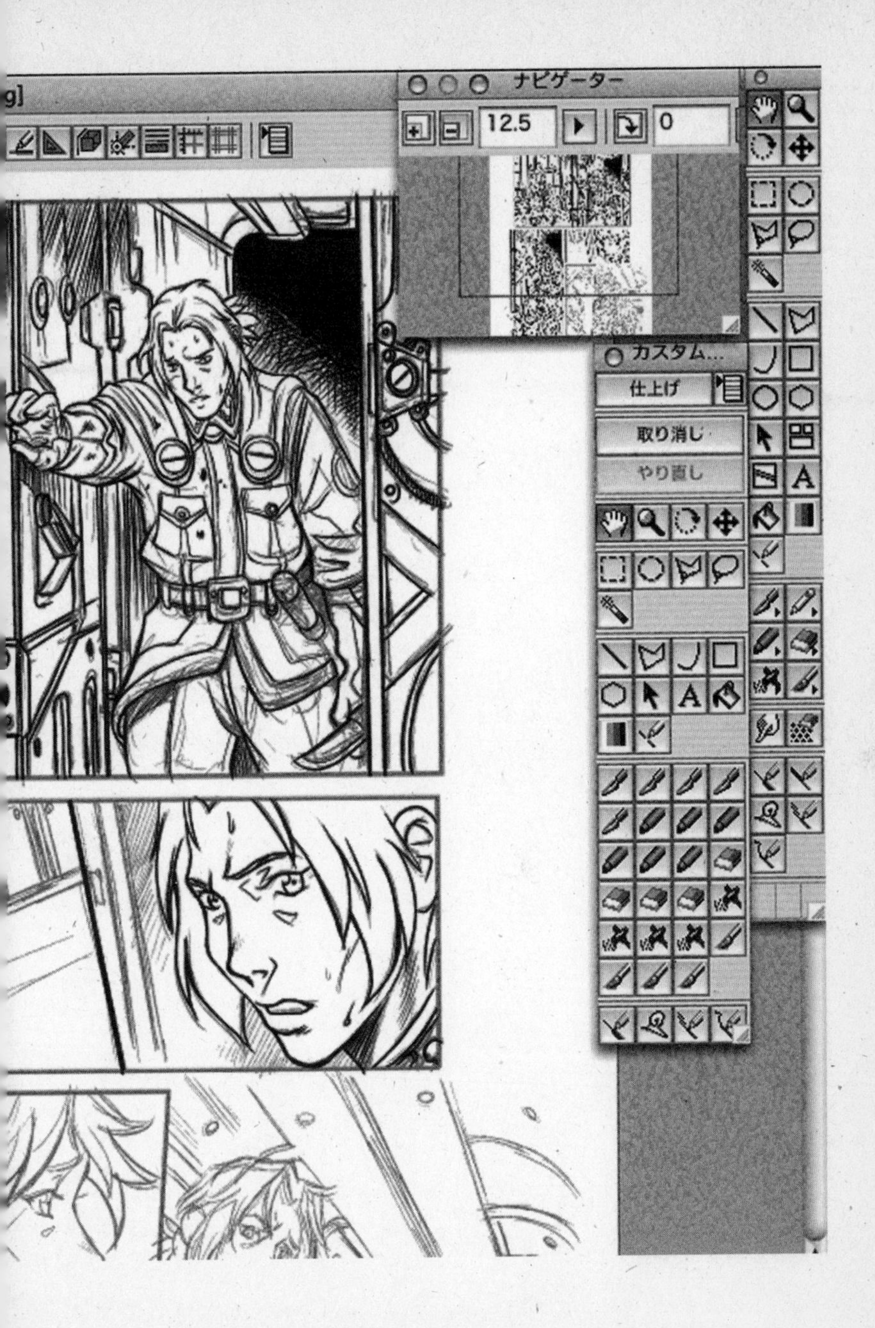
ナビゲーター
12.5
0
カスタム...
仕上げ
取り消し
やり直し

PAGE THIRTY-EIGHT

Panel One
Lady Macbeth nearly jumps out of her skin as a voice emanated from behind a secret door.

BALLOON: FROM BEHIND THE SECRET DOOR
Who's there? What, ho?

Panel Two
But Lady Macbeth is disoriented; she does not realize the source of the voice. She is looking about, perhaps to the ceiling or the sky, but definitely not toward the door.

BALLOON: LADY MACBETH
Alack, I am afraid they have awaked,
And 'tis not done. Th' attempt, and not the deed,
Confounds us. Hark!

Panel Three
Lady Macbeth in the king's guest room, as the king and the servants sleep. She is putting the servant's daggers in plain sight.

CAPTION:
"I laid their daggers ready –
He could not miss 'em."

Panel Four
She is still in the chamber; she is looking down at the king with a conflicted expression.

CAPTION:
"Had he not resembled
My father as he slept, I had done't.

A copy of page 38 of Arthur's script. Note that he includes art instructions as well as the dialogue.

Tony's art for page 38.

A copy of the first rough cover sketch Tony submitted for *Macbeth.*

A copy of the finished pencil art for the cover that incorporates the editorial feedback. Though the overall composition remains the same, there are some small differences. Compare this version with the earlier sketch.

WILLIAM SHAKESPEARE is regarded as the greatest writer in the English language. Though his plays are world famous, very little is actually known about him. In fact, there are two periods in his life, 1578–82 and 1585–92, known as the "lost years" in which absolutely nothing is known.

Shakespeare was born to a prominent family in Stratford, England, in 1564, the third of seven children. He moved to London as an adult and there he made his mark not only as a playwright, but also as an actor and a poet. When he died in 1616, he had composed 37 plays and 154 sonnets. Shakespeare was a writer of incredible range. He penned everything from romances (*Romeo and Juliet*), to comedies (*Twelfth Night*), to tragedies (*Macbeth*), and histories (*Henry V*). A number of phrases and expressions used today, including "salad days" and "it was Greek to me" originally appeared in Shakespeare's plays. His plays continue to be performed both on the stage in amateur and professional productions and in movies.

TONY LEONARD TAMAI, a graphic designer and illustrator, has been drawing comics since his teens, and was weaned at an early age on cult films, Eurocomics, and hardboiled Japanese manga. Tamai is currently working on developing his own titles, as well as conceptual and commercial illustrations. His experimental web-publishing site may be found at www.tonikoro.com. Recently relocated from Los Angeles, Tamai lives with his wife and family in Nagoya, Japan.

ARTHUR BYRON COVER was born in the upper tundra of Siberia in 1950. He attended a Clarion Science Fiction Writer's workshop in 1971 where he made his first professional sale to Harlan Ellison's *Last Dangerous Visions*. Cover has published a slew of short stories, in *Infinity Five*, *The Alien Condition*, *Heavy Metal*, *Weird Tales*, *Year's Best Horror Stories*, and elsewhere, plus several science fiction novels. He has written scripts for the comic books *Daredevil* and *Firestorm*, as well as the graphic novel *Space Clusters*. Among his most recent projects have been his bestselling novelization of the comic book series J. Michael Straczynski's *Rising Stars*, and the novelization of Archangel Studios' *The Red Star* graphic novel series. He currently resides in California.